MW01107520

DangerRAMA
By Danger_Slater

Edited By Arthur Gelsinger

Cover Art By April Guadiana

Joseph,
Wherever you go,
Whatever you do
Don't forget to get
"Jiggy" with it.

thanks,

Will ~~Smith~~ errr...
I mean...

Danger Slater

This book is a work of fiction. Any resemblance to actual events, locales, or persons living or dead is purely coincidental.

Copyright © 2013 Rooster Republic Press

DangerRAMA

ISBN 10: 0615837298

ISBN 13: 978-0615837291

All rights reserved. No part of this book may be used or reproduced in any manner whatsoever without written permission from the publisher, except in the case of brief quotations embodied in articles and reviews.

Published 2013 by Rooster Republic Press
www.roosterrepublicpress.com

Contents

KNIGHTS OF THE WHITE CASTLE

a novella by Danger_Slater

CHAPTER 1

There's a pause –

A long, uncomfortable pause.

A long, uncomfortable pause that fills the air between us like cigar smoke. Asphyxiating, tangible, all-encompassing. This is the kind of pause that hangs there like a crooked painting on the wall – one of those perfectly artful moments of awkwardness that can only be achieved when you're just sort of staring at the girl behind the counter of your local White Castle and she's just sort of standing there staring back at you and you're both staring at each other and nobody blinks and "Across the Universe" by The Beatles is playing faintly over the sound system but neither of you are paying any attention to that because you're indefatigably locked in this Mexican standoff of befuddled stares.

It's one of *those* kind of pauses.

So what's the deal here, huh? Am I dead? Being punished by God? Have I woken up in my own personal hell? I'm sure the devil would have a difficult time conceiving a more heinous torture than locking me eternally in this horrid moment – forever forcing me to gaze at this ghastly girl's greasy, judgmental face.

"You tellin' me you want 47 hamburgers, all fo' yo'self?" she finally says after what felt like ten-thousand millennia. All 300 pounds of her elephantine frame seem to have climbed up her forehead and are now regarding me from the perilous perch above her one flummoxed eyebrow. I am left with no choice but to flummox an eyebrow back and note her with scorn: the mongoloid slack

1

of her open jaw, the half-there look in her glassy eyes, the nametag pinned upon her cartoonishly-large bosom that reads, in sloppy bold-faced lettering, HI MY NAME IS EARTHA HOW MAY I HELP YOU?

"Eartha," I coo, gently cupping her chubby hand in mine, "I know this must be a very difficult job you have here. I'm not going to pretend I understand all the subtle intricacies and nuances that one must master in this line of work: button pushing! Second grade math! Drive-thru etiquette! *Whew*! I'm exhausted just thinking about it! It's a good thing that there are dedicated professionals, such as yourself, who have taken the time and effort to learn the complex ins and outs of the fast food industry. Of course, seeing as how you've failed to successfully take my order thus far, a task in which you've invested so much of yourself in learning, I can only assume you have even GREATER things going on in that noggin of yours. But what, I'm left to ponder, could be more important than the customer – me – that stands before you right now? *Hmmm*...I wonder...did you just come up with a cure for cancer? Could you be mentally penning a massive tome of iambic love sonnets? Or perhaps you're working on a polydimensional time-traveling device in the back office? Is that what's happening, Eartha? Are you on the verge of perfecting polydimensional time-travel?"

Now she's staring at me like I'm toxic. Like I'm on fire.

"Um...no..." she says.

"Oh!" I release her hand, "That's funny because it just so happens that I *AM* on the verge of finishing a polydimensional time-traveling device. And since you probably don't understand the subtle intricacies and nuances that come with *that*, I think it's safe to assume that you are not aware that GREAT GENIUS such as mine requires GREAT FUEL to efficiently operate. Now Eartha, as the purveyor of the aforementioned fuel, you play an integral part in this very delicate process. To impede me with your inane line of questioning, coupled with the fact that we've been standing here for 10 minutes having this little parlay, could only mean one of two things: 1) you sincerely didn't hear me when I ordered, which, considering your previous vocal inflections and that stupid fucking look you've been giving me since I got here, I can safely conclude is not the case, or 2) you're trying to thwart my efforts through whatever nefarious means you can. As such, my dear, you must know this entire conversation has not only been an affront to me personally, but also an affront to the future generations my work will surely benefit. Now, you're a smart girl, Eartha. We've already established that, right? So as a smart girl, I

KNOW you don't want to be the one single person who robs the human race of the glory I'm about to bestow upon it. Do you?"

She shakes her head no.

"Of course you don't," I continue. "Who would, right? So here's what I suggest you do: first, you're going to reach down to that keyboard there with that fat little mitten you call a hand. Next, you're going to press the button with the drawing of a hamburger on it 47 fucking times. And finally, you are going to give me my GODDAMN FOOD!"

Honestly, I didn't mean to yell at her, but right now I have no time for such banalities. I also have no time for sleep, friendships or basic hygiene. I'm a busy, busy man and I didn't come in here for an inquisition.

I came in here to eat.

She puts in my order. The computer beeps. Onscreen a message flashes. I can see it reflecting in the oiliest parts of her chin. She gulps, looks up at me with fearful eyes and reluctantly asks the question that every fast-food employee is duty-bound to ask:

"Do you want fries with that?"

"What do you think, Eartha?" I sigh. "Of course I do!"

CHAPTER TWO

The burgers are stacked high. All 47 of them. Each tiny slider housed in its own little box. Meticulously placed on the blue plastic tray, brick by brick. Arranged like a pyramid. I stand above them like I'm the King of the Moon.

Like it is I who control the tides.

I'm so close to completing my device. Just the twist of a screw or the tweak of a decimal and then it'll be I, Dr. Phineus Dracon – scourge of the scientific community, bane of Hanover Middle School's physics department – who will have the last laugh! And what, you're probably asking yourself, is a guy like me going to do once he's able to harness the AWESOME powers of TIME ITSELF? The answer is simple. I will only claim what should already be mine. Appreciation. Veneration. Vindication. Exaltation. I will travel. I will travel FAR into the future, FAR away from the legions of dipshits and window-lickers that constantly surround me, FAR FAR away, where a more enlightened society will be there to greet me and, of course, shower me with the praise and accolades a genius like mine so clearly deserves. They'll worship me. Perhaps they'll make me their emperor. Their president. Their pharaoh. I'll have a supermodel wife. I'll be rich. I'll be famous. I'll be loved and lauded by everyone around me. And I'll start sending cryptic messages backwards through the aether to be received by all those halfwits and skeptics who so callously mocked my unequivocally brilliant ideas and shunned me from their so-called "scientific community."

I TOLD YOU SO, is all my message would say. I TOLD YOU SO! BWA-HA-HA-HA-HA...

But, before all that, I'm going to need some brain food. And if my former research has not led me astray, it will take *exactly* 47 White Castle hamburgers and a side of fries to provide me with the proper sustenance I need to finally complete my project.

KNIGHTS OF THE WHITE CASTLE

CHAPTER THREE

Of course, before I can even begin my meal, the boorishness and fuckwittery of our hapless modern culture once again manifests itself, this time as a group of nearby teenagers snickering at me.

I turn to the puffy-eyed cavalcade and immediately recognize one of the faces.

"Is something funny to you, Mr. Schaffer?" I ask the boy seated closest.

Lance Schaffer. A former student of mine. Not exactly the brightest light bulb on the chandelier, if you know what I mean. I can't recall him ever scoring above a C, even on the most rudimentary of exams. But he was well-known and well-liked amongst the other students, though I'll never understand why. I guess if you consider constantly disrespecting your educators by making fart sounds with the crook of your arm to be the quintessence of wit, then *maybe* you and Lance might get along. Then again, you're probably just as stupid as he is. Middle school *should* be about two things and two things only: applying yourself academically and trying to hide awkward study hall boners. It is NOT a popularity contest. It's your first step on the road to adulthood. But no, no, no – not for Lance Schaffer. Lance was too busy being "good-looking" and "popular" to play by the rules or pay any attention to what a "stuff-shirt" old teacher like me had to say. Even if what I was saying was LIFE-ALTERINGLY, MIND-BLOWINGLY, EARTH-SHATTERINGLY BRILLIANT!

When I mention his name it sends the group into another giggle-fit.

"What is so funny? Have you been smoking drugs, Mr. Schaffer?" I scold him.

"No sir, Mr. Dracon," he replies in a mock-nasal voice, which I assume is supposed to mimic my own. A deviated septum is a serious medical condition and should not be the butt of his insolent attempt at a joke. Of course, that doesn't stop his idiotic friends from chuckling along with him. One of them, a pretty blonde girl, keeps burying her head into his neck. A single blue eye peeks out from in between wisps of honey-yellow hair as she snorts and giggles into her boyfriend's nape.

"Well then I must be missing something," I say, "because I don't see anything humorous about randomly running into one of your former middle school teachers eating a ludicrous amount of White Castle hamburgers at one in the morning on a Tuesday."

Lance whispers something into the blonde girl's ear.

"I can't..." she protests with a flirtatious smile.

"C'mon," he goads her with a light shove, pointing towards me, "what's he gonna do?"

She looks up at me with her robin egg-blue eyes and clears her throat. "So...um...Lance tells me you got fired for burning down the school."

The boy seated across from them breaks out into peels of uncontrollable laughter.

"Well, Miss..."

"Sally," she says.

"Well, Miss Sally," I say, "Contrary to what the local news-media would have you believe, I did NOT burn down the school. It was only one room. And it was an accident. Of course, the *plebeians* in the P.T.A. couldn't appreciate the big picture, now could they? As with any endeavor worth undertaking, a certain amount of...expendable losses...can be expected to incur. Greatness comes with a hefty price tag, my dear. A price I unfortunately paid for with my tenure."

"My dad says you're a lunatic and you should be locked up," says the unnamed boy.

"Is that a fact?" I ask, rage flowing through me like rattlesnake venom. "Well you know what *I* think? I think that YOUR DAD CAN GO DROWN HIMSELF IN A SWIMMING POOL FULL OF DICKS!"

This shuts him up quick.

6

I get even more rattlesnakey as I lean in towards them. "Oh what? Surprised a teacher can say 'dicks?' Well I got news for you kids: DICKS DICKS DICKS DICKS DICKS DICKS DICKS DICKS DICKS!"

And now I'm being stared at by all three teenagers. Even Eartha behind the counter is eyeballing me dubiously.

"NOW, if you'll all excuse me," I say to everyone in the restaurant, "my dinner is getting cold."

CHAPTER FOUR

Once that's settled, I return to my feast.

The scent of the meat waltzes its way through the stale dining room air to climb up my nostrils and dance with my nose hair. It hits me like a shot of Thorazine. I am immediately calmed.

I pick up the first sandwich, its miniature bun aesthetically sound in the palm of my hand, perfectly contoured to it like a baseball. Slowly, I raise it up to my lips. And just as I'm about to bite down, just as I'm about to let the onions, mayo, mustard and cheddar pervert my tongue with their dirty disco of flavor, just as I'm about to feed my stomach and feed my soul – the doors burst open and in storms a man dressed up as a knight.

A blood-spattered X crosses his lion-crested breastplate and his greaves are caked in mud and mire. His armor rattles like maracas as he clomps lead-footed across the linoleum. His gait is swift and purposeful, like a freight train, knocking aside tables and chairs in his wake. With a single swipe of matte-gray steel, he carelessly capsizes the banquet I had just laid out for myself. My burgers go tumbling to the grime-slick floor.

"Oh for Pete's sake," I huff. "What is this, Everybody-Prevent-Doctor-Phineus-Dracon-From-Enjoying-His-Supper Day?"

The knight advances upon the front counter, pulling his helmet visor up as he approaches Eartha.

"What in the name of the Lord's dew-born dawn is happening to me?!?" he cries, violently retching.

"I don' know what yo' problem is, Lancelot, but I'd prefer if it were happenin' outside," she replies.

The knight stumbles back a step as if drunk, seeming to sway in a breeze only he can feel. His pale-blue eyes are wide, full of fear and wonderment, as he takes in his surroundings. The anemic flicker of dim fluorescent lights. The serpentine hiss of burgers overcooking. The soda machine to his left quietly clicks as it finishes making some ice.

8

Startled, he lets out a yelp, draws his sword, and stabs clean through the soft drink dispenser. Pepsi Max squirts out like blood to form a syrupy pool on the tiled floor.

"C'mon, bro," Eartha halfheartedly protests. "You know I gotta clean that shit up."

Lance and his friends resume laughing.

"Hahaha," Lance's tomato-faced comrade titters through labored breaths, "what the fuck is going on?"

"Shut up, shut up! He can hear you," Lance snickers, tears of hilarity welling up in his eyes.

The knight turns his attention upon them. He growls as he clambers through the overturned chairs and tables, squashing my burgers even flatter in the process. He grabs Lance by his collar and slams him down onto the table in one clean motion.

"What brings thee to such hysterics, thou satin-livered ninny?" the knight demands.

His insult only incites them further.

"Oh jeez!" Lance squeals sarcastically. "He's got me now! Look out! Hahaha! I'm in trouble!"

"Yeah," his friend chimes in, "you're in trouble all right, thou satin-livered nin—"

The knight swings his blade, decapitating the boy before he can even finish his smart-alecky sentence. Garnet-red blood and stippled, sinewy gore erupt from his neck as his head rolls across the floor, splashing through the growing puddle of Mountain Dew now leaking from the soda machine, eventually stopping at Eartha's feet.

She dry heaves. Miss Sally screams. Lance's confidence dissolves faster than the piss now saturating the front of his pants.

Ha! Not so 'cool' now, are we Mr. Schaffer?

"Don't kill me don't kill me OHPLEASEGOD don't kill me!" Lance begs the beleaguered knight.

"Be a man and greet thy maker with thine dignity intact!" cries the noble paladin, raising his sword for the final, fatal strike.

I sigh.

"Wait," I begrudgingly interrupt. "As much as I'd like to see you decollate this unabashed rube's arrogant head, I must assume that playing witness to a mass murder, however innocent my part may be, would do nothing to rectify my already impugned reputation."

The knight releases Lance and turns towards me.

"We all just need to relax," I continue. "Let's regain some civility here. Deep breaths, in and out. *MMmmm. AAhhh.* Now, just who are you, friend?" I ask him.

"I am Sir Jonas the Valiant," he booms. "And who might you be, O Brave One with the Razor Tongue?"

"Me? I – um – I am...Sir Phineus...of Hanover." I play along. "And I demand that you relinquish your siege."

The knight slowly steps up to me until we're just a few inches apart, his face in mine, consuming the whole of my vision. All I can see are his cold, indigo eyes, immobile in their icy stare. Like a wounded wolf, he looks at me. Into me.

He slowly raises his sword to my throat. I dare not swallow lest I receive an amateur tracheotomy. But even in this most dire of moments, I still do not flinch. And I do not back down. I was a middle school teacher for 11 years, after all. This is nothing.

Soon enough, his chiseled countenance begins to waver. His lip starts to tremble and his eyes glaze over. A flood of emotions rages within him. Like a dam about to burst, the pressure just builds and builds...

...until it eventually cracks.

CHAPTER FIVE

"Alas!" he bellows, collapsing backwards into a chair. He pulls his helmet off and lets it fall to the ground. The wrinkles on his forehead spell duress, consternation like railroad tracks crisscrossing his brow. All the thunder and gallantry he previously commanded now gone. He speaks in docile, candid tones, no more imposing than a passive pussycat. This is a man in the thralls of shock. Of panic. A man defeated. A man afraid.

"I fear some wicked alchemy has been cast upon me," he quavers through trembling lips. "I find myself lost into these strange new surroundings without provocation nor cause to herald my arrival. One moment I am storming the palace at Wiltshire in the name of my kingdom, and the next I am...thrust...through some kind of...*portal*. I don't know how to explain it. 'Twas like a hole you can only see if you're not looking. Like a fissure, a crack, in the very air itself. All of a sudden I was enveloped in light. Consumed by light. Ages seemed to pass. Untold amounts of time. I blacked out, the experience too overwhelming. When I came to, I found myself on the side of a long, black trail, hardened like stone yet flat as the most placid of ponds. A nearby signpost proclaimed the pathway as Route 46. I – I wandered down it, aimless in my pursuit, for I knew not where I was, nor what devilry these mechanized, horseless carriages portended. They recklessly flew past at speeds heretofore unknown! Like lightning. Like shooting stars.... I searched – O Dear Lord, hours I searched! – for any familiar vestiges to help guide me on my way. It was then that I happened upon this hallowed spot. A castle! A White Castle! O sweet respite, thank you! I have come to beseech your lord for mercy."

"There ain't no lords here," says Eartha. "This here's a hamburger joint."

"I am in Hamburg?" the knight asks incredulously.

"No, you're in New Jersey," I tell him.

"Please," he says, abruptly standing. "My liege and my kingdom await! The evil King Schaffer's army marches even as we speak!"

"Schaffer?" Lance absentmindedly blurts, "Schaffer is my last name."

Sir Jonas draws his sword.

"Hold up," I say, sliding in between the two, "It's obvious to me that Sir Jonas here must've had one too many 'goblets' of 'mead' at the Ye Olde Renaissance Faire."

"Good Sir Phineus, I know not of this 'Faire' of which you speak. Now step aside so that I may slay this dastardly fiend!"

He points his sword over my shoulder threateningly at Lance.

"No! There will be no more slaying today!" I tell him. "Sir Jonas, my good knight, you're obviously suffering from some sort of delusional psychosis. A mental break, if you will. But it doesn't necessarily mean you're 'crazy.' You just need to calm down a bit. Get your bearings straight. Let's start simple: why don't you tell us what year you think it is?"

"Is this some sort of ruse?" he says. "I have not the patience for this jackassery, sir. It is October the 26th, *anno domini*, 1378."

"*Pfffft,*" Lance scoffs, peeking out from behind me, "Yeah. Okay, dude. What's he gonna tell us next, he traveled through time?"

"Settle down, Mr. Schaffer, and please don't agitate him any further," I say. "Plus, it's not very nice to make fun of the mentally handi...capped..."

I trail off as something occurs to me. It seems unlikely, but what if this knight is telling the truth? What if he really *is* from the past?

No! Banish the thought!

But *what if...*?

Thoughts begin orbiting around in my head like satellites. Could it be? But how? Who? What? Where? When? And, most importantly, why? Faster and faster these ideas spin until my mind is just a blur. My adrenaline surges. And I tingle. And I'm numb. My heartbeat echoes in my eardrums as everything gradually falls into focus.

My machine...it...it...

KNIGHTS OF THE WHITE CASTLE

"It WORKED!"

CHAPTER SIX

At my behest (and on my dime) Eartha brings Sir Jonas a tray of food. The knight shovels it down his throat by the handful, barely chewing as he swallows.

"Mmmph," he grunts through his greasy, smacking lips. "What do you call these things again?"

"You mean the chicken rings?" Eartha asks.

"Chicken in *ring* form!" Sir Jonas exclaims. "This surely is a most peculiar place!"

"I don't understand," I mutter to myself, pacing before my teenage audience. I fiddle clumsily with my hands like I have all these extra fingers I don't know what to do with. "How is this even possible? The Infinity Unit was not calibrated...the Hyper-Dimensional Capacitor was not charged...there was still so much work to do! It was simply not ready."

"What are you blabbering about, old man?" goes Lance.

I turn to my former student.

"I'm afraid something has gone terribly wrong."

"Well *that's* the understatement of the year!" he says, motioning to his headless friend, bleeding out in the corner of the dining room.

"Mr. Schaffer, if my calculations are correct, death may be the least of our problems."

Eartha approaches me.

"Um...Mr. Dracon?"

"That's *Doctor* Dracon, Eartha. D-o-c-t-o-r! And why are you bothering me right now? Are you out of Fish Nibblers or something?"

14

"No, we still have plenty 'a Fish Nibblers. It's juss...somethin' happened..."

"Yes? Well, spit it out, you blubbering whale! I haven't got all night. Can't you see that I'm in the middle of some pretty serious conjecture over here? Jeez!"

"It's juss that...well, I went to call the cops, ya know, to get all you crazy people outta my store, but when I picked up the phone it...turned into a pumpkin."

"Ah, the fall harvest," goes Sir Jonas. "Just in time for the All Hallows celebration. Resplendent!"

"Wait, what do you mean 'a pumpkin'?" Miss Sally nervously asks.

"What I mean is that the motherfuckin' telephone turned into a MOTHERFUCKIN' PUMPKIN!" Eartha cries out.

"Oh no," I groan. "No no no no no no no no no no no no no no no no no no no..."

Flipping over a napkin, I scribble a few equations on the back. I redo the work in my head, making sure I've carried all the ones and rooted all the squares. The math doesn't lie.

"No no no. This can't be happening..."

"Spit it out, dude," says Lance. "What are you getting at?"

"It's the space/time continuum, you fucking moron!" I shout at him. "My machine wasn't ready. The Paradox Drive has malfunctioned. We were too late to stop it. The paradox has already occurred! Maybe if you hadn't slept through my advanced theoretical hypospace derivatives lectures, Mr. Schaffer, you'd have an inkling about how serious this is."

"Yo, whatever dude," Lance brushes me off. "You think I need this kinda shit right now? I just saw my friend get his head chopped off. This whole night has been just one long, bad trip and it's bugging me the hell out. That weed musta been laced or something. Last time I buy bud from freakin' Harland, I'll tell you that much." He turns to Miss Sally. "C'mon, let's just go back to my place and sleep it off. I'm sure everything'll be back to normal in the morning."

He takes her hand into his and stands. I step between them and the exit, blocking their path.

"There is no 'normal' anymore, Mr. Schaffer. Please sit back down."

"Get the hell out of my way, you geriatric fuck! Quit trying to pull everyone else into your own craziness."

"Mr. Schaffer, I implore you. We must stay within the radian of the nexus or else the consequences will surely be dire."

"Speak English, you douche," he says.

"We must stay within the radian of the nexus," I repeat. "I don't know how I can be any clearer than that."

"Maybe we should just wait a minute," suggests Miss Sally.

"Listen to me," I say, "We've tampered with history. The paradox has happened. Do you realize the implications? Have you ever heard of the butterfly effect? By removing Sir Jonas from the past, we have changed *everything*."

"*We* didn't do anything," Lance says of himself and Miss Sally. "*We* got stoned and went out for some burgers. That's it. You're the one who's fucking up the 'space/time condominium' or whatever it's called."

"Let me try to put this in terms you'll understand," I say. "History is like a pyramid. And every moment in that history is like a brick. The present – right now – is the top of that pyramid. A minute ago was like the layer of bricks beneath that. Two minutes ago was the layer beneath that. And so on and so on and the farther back you go – the lower down the pyramid you travel – the wider the structure becomes, right? It is all those moments, all those bricks, that hold the top of the pyramid in place, that allow the present to exist as we know it. The question is, what do you think happens when a brick is removed?"

"Um...you talk for a really long time about some boring bullshit?" Lance replies.

I point to the trampled pile of hamburgers on the floor.

"The pyramid collapses!" I say. "The Paradox Drive was meant to fill in that empty space. To hold everything firmly in place. Without it, the Universe will try and correct itself. To hammer out the anachronism. Everything from that point in history has changed. All those bricks – they have split off and begun to form their own pyramids. Parallel dimensions. And the longer Sir Jonas is here, the worse it will undoubtedly get. He is the vertex on which our entire 'reality' is hinged. We must stay within his immediate vicinity until he is returned back to his own time. Or else..."

"Or else what?" goes Eartha.

"Or else, who knows! The structural integrity of the entire Universe is out of whack! I mean this quite literally: ANYTHING and EVERYTHING can happen!"

"Oh God," the knight suddenly interrupts, his eyes rolled back in ecstasy. "What do you call this red stuff again? Ketchup? It's delicious!"

CHAPTER SEVEN

Suddenly, the whole Earth shakes.

I brace myself against a table. Miss Sally clamps onto Lance, her French-tipped nails digging deep into his shoulder. I see another spot of wetness forming in the crotch of his pants.

Gross, Mr. Schaffer. Gross.

Outside, along the dark edge of the distant horizon, a streak of silver light rips across the sky with a thunderous roar, like jet engines or timpani drums or a hundred-thousand zippers all unzippering at once! Like burning paper, the night grows blacker and more sinister against the blinding white opening. The sky peels back. Waves of swirling blues and reds and greens and purples spontaneously pour forth – entwined like nebulas so brilliant it's as if we were witnessing the birth of the stars themselves.

Like liquid the light flows quickly towards us, over hills and along valleys. It crosses the highway outside, devouring all in its path.

And then we're inside it.

I see color. I see every color AT THE EXACT SAME TIME! I see colors that don't even exist, that don't have names, that are beyond all perception, description or imagination – and I'm drowning in them. I'm drowning in the fluorescent ocean of time. My body is being stretched and pulled like taffy. Minutes, hours, days, years, decades, centuries, and eons and eons and eons and eons – time loses all meaning as it tangles itself up like a helix. Where am I? When am I? WHAT am I?

My hair grows quickly, turns gray and falls out. Fingernails burgeon, then yellow and break off, and my teeth turn to slime as they rot out of my mouth. I'm an old man. I'm dying. I'm dead. I'm dust. But in an instant I am reborn! I'm me again! A baby, soft and pink and the whole world is new! Then I'm a toddler. Then a teenager. Then a man. Then an old man. Then I'm dead again. Then reborn. Dead again. Reborn. Dead again, reborn. Dead, reborn. Dead, born. Dead born. Dead born. Dead born dead born dead born dddee bbbbe eddde ebbbeddddbbbbdbdbdbdbdb...

Until...

The wave passes.

"What the fuck *was* that?!?" Lance cries out.

"I suspect that was just the first of an increasing number of continuity waves – confluences of concentrated possibility – most likely being expelled from the site of the interdimensional rift. If we're going to have any chance at stopping this thing, that's where we need to go."

"But Dr. Dracon, how are we supposed to know where this interdimensional rift is?" Miss Sally asks.

"Easy," I tell her. "It's about 11 miles east of here."

"Now how could you possibly know that?" Lance demands, turning towards me.

"Simple, Mr. Schaffer," I reply, "because that's where my house is."

"Um...guys," Eartha interrupts, "I think y'all gonna wanna see this..." Her face is pressed up against the restaurant's front window and her hot breath paints the treated glass a foreboding shade of gray.

"It's called a reflection, Eartha, and everybody has one," I say with a chuckle, patting her head reassuringly as I wipe her stinky mouth-fog off the window.

And then I see what she's gawking at. "Oh shit," is all I can manage to say.

The McDonald's restaurant across the street has transformed into a blacksmiths. The iconic 'golden arches' have been replaced by two downturned horseshoes. The 'playland' is now a scrapyard of piece metal. A thatched-grass eave is what the drive-thru awning has become, and beneath that a square-faced man stands, pounding an iron pike against an anvil. *Ponk ponk ponk* his hammer goes, spitting out sparks into the surrounding darkness.

"It's happening," I whisper in a throaty drawl.

"Is that Old McDonald?" asks Sir Jonas, squinting.

The knight waves hello. The blacksmith amicably waves back.

"It is! Fantastic! Haha. You know, Old McDonald had a farm," he says.

Lance can't help but snicker. Sir Jonas looks at the boy with confusion.

"What is so funny?" asks Sir Jonas. "Old McDonald did have a farm. Before he became a blacksmith."

Lance laughs even harder.

"We need to get back to the time machine," I say, "And I mean NOW."

"And on his farm he has some ducks," Sir Jonas continues.

"EE-I-EE-I-O," I add, gravely.

CHAPTER EIGHT

"Everyone, stay close," I tell the group as we make like a conga line through the parking lot. My car sits at the opposite end. "No sudden movements. Keep in formation."

Our pace is slow. Cautious. Calculated, as I always am.

It is deceptively quiet outside. Like the calm before a hurricane, or the reading room in a library. Something just felt...wrong.

With each step forward, the blacktop seems to get less solid underfoot. Less like a blacktop and more like a waterbed. Softer. Doughier. More malleable. It's like walking on the skin of a bruised-up orange, or traversing a field of that disgusting, semi-viscous gunk that forms on the top of three-day-old pudding. We are pudding-walking across the parking lot.

There is a dull sort of heat radiating from the ground beneath us. Not a fiery kind of heat, but faint. Cigarette heat. E-Z Bake oven heat. And the further we progress, the hotter it gets.

And then, up ahead, I can see the asphalt begin to buckle and pulsate, like it's dancing to its own secret song. It balloons out and up, forming a crusty black bubble. The bubble gets bigger, and bigger, and BIGGER! A pillar of volcanic flame suddenly bursts through the tarmac. Nearby cars sink into the asphalt as the ground grows even less stable.

"Has the parking lot always been this squishy...and explosive?" asks Lance, pulling his leg up out of the ever-softening muck.

"Nah," says Eartha, "Far as I can remember, it's usually pretty sturdy."

"*Hmmm*," I say. "Reverse geothermal petrifaction, I suspect."

This only elicits sideways looks. I sigh.

"It's reverting back to tar," I explain.

"Oh, of course!" Lance mocks me once again. "Reverse geometric putrefaction, or whatever you just said. How could we not have known that!"

"Tease me all you like, Mr. Schaffer. It doesn't change the fact that you're sinking."

Lance is now up to his knees in the tar pit.

"Aw fuck, man. These are new Jordans. Someone get me out of this crap!"

He grabs onto Eartha and tries to pull himself up.

"Get the hell offa me!" she screams as he drags her equator-deep into the sludge.

"I'm gonna die in a White Castle parking lot, aren't I?" Miss Sally cries. "OMG, this is so embarrassing!"

"Don't fret, milady," Sir Jonas gallantly crows, scooping her out of her ballet flats and into his arms. The shoes go upright and sink into the goop like size-7 shipwrecks.

"Whoa," she swoons. "I guess chivalry isn't dead..."

Lance growls at Sir Jonas. The knight doesn't even notice. The tar continues to warm up. Getting softer and stickier. We continue to sink.

"Well c'mon, grandpa. Do something!" Eartha begs as a pocket of small bubbles surface behind her, a sign that either the asphalt has reached its boiling point, or she's just farted.

Then the smell hits me.

"What do you expect ME to do?" I ask, motioning to my own tar-deep nipples.

"I don' freakin' know," she goes, "you're the doctor!"

"Yeah, I'm a doctor, Eartha. Of quantum physics. Not MOTHERFUCKING GEOLOGY, YOU BARKING MOOSE!"

KNIGHTS OF THE WHITE CASTLE

"So what are you saying? We're stuck?" goes Lance.

"A very astute observation, Mr. Schaffer. Any more pearls of wisdom?"

"Yeah. You're a dickhead," he adds.

Suddenly, a loud, piercing shriek calls our attention skyward.

SSSCraw! it echoes through the night, slicing like a razor blade into the lowest point of my spine. Thoughts of a slow, painful death by drowning in this smelted sludge are in turn replaced by thoughts of a slow, painful death at the mercy of the hungry-looking pterodactyl now circling overhead.

The wings of the beast stretch at least 30 feet wide, suffocating the prevailing moonlight like a rainforest canopy. Its obsidian gaze zeros in on our location; malevolent, beady eyes following the slow descent of our bodies into the tar.

SSSCraw! SSSCraw!

"Great. It's a fucking dinosaur," huffs Lance. "I should've guessed, right? Anything's possible, eh? So what's next then? A rapping T-Rex?

"Yo yo yo," a Tyrannosaurus Rex calls out to us from the tar-pit's opposite shore.

"Oh noooo," Lance groans.

The T-Rex smiles at us, revealing a platinum-plated grill of scissor-sharp teeth. Next to him is a Triceratops wearing dark shades, a backwards White Sox cap, and an oversized clock necklace.

The Triceratops starts to beatbox. The T-Rex nods along. He's feeling the groove.

And then he starts freestyling:

Yo, I'm the T-Rex and I'll eat ya face.

23

Danger_Slater

Nothing can stop me, son, not even a mace.

I'll put y'all in ya place

An' leave not a trace.

Cause you people are weak, yo, and have such a yummy taste!

SSSCraw! the pterodactyl cries out, rapping back in reply:

T-Rex? More like Beavis. Ya think ya can beat this?

You're justa big pussy with a little penis.

I saw these fools first.

For their blood I do thirst.

An' if you challenge me you'll go home in a hearse!

The Tyrannosaurus roars before volleying back:

Keep squawkin'. Keep talkin'. You ain't fly. You walkin'.

You think you a hawk when you more like a cock and

You ain't got nuttin' on me.

You're just a disease.

I'm da King of Swing bitch, so get on yo' knees.

KNIGHTS OF THE WHITE CASTLE

The pterodactyl is nonplussed:

For all your huffin' and puffin' you don't bring nothin'.

You think I'ma turkey? Well then my words are the stuffin'.

And you know I ain't bluffin'.

It's yo ass I'll be snuffin'.

You think I'm rough now? Bitch, this is just fluffin'.

The T-Rex just shakes his head and chuckles:

You stupid pterodactyl. I'm the battle master.

You betta back yo' ass up or you'll leave a disaster.

I'll lay ya flat on your back

Then rip off your nutsack.

Cause your shit is so wack I'll just have you for a snack!

"Oh snap!" says Lance.

"Quite the bard, that thunderbeast is," Sir Jonas agrees.

And with that the T-Rex leaps into the air and chomps the flying pterosaur in mid flight.

Danger_Slater

SSSCrawffffuck! the pterodactyl screams out in agony. The tyrannosaur clenches his teeth. Bones pop like firecrackers as chunks of flesh and sanguine viscera spill forth. The T-Rex lands back on the tar-pit's shore, but his balance has been thrown off by the thrashing winged creature in his jaws. He rears up on one foot, perilously hovering over the molten black soup. His tiny arms futilely flail as he falls.

"Oh shizzz! WestKoastDinoZKrew-4-EVA!" are the T-Rex's last words before he splashes, headfirst, into the tar.

A tremendous wave of liquefied asphalt rolls towards us, sweeping us away in the churning morass. Into the blanket of boiling bitumen we are pulled, future fossil fuels just waiting to happen. Somehow I resurface. I claw at the air like I'm going to strangle the breeze and force it into my lungs. And then I'm under again. Like fragments of a broken seashell, we are helpless against the force of the surf. We go where we are carried; there is no fighting it. We survive or die by simple chance. There's my Honda Civic, just slightly ahead. Still intact and on solid ground. It's a miracle! If only I...could...make it over there.

With all my strength I swim. I windmill my arms like sledgehammers, SLOWLY paddling my way through the muck. Fighting the tide. Finally, I am close enough that I can grab onto the car's bumper with one hand. I hold onto Sir Jonas with the other. Sir Jonas holds onto Miss Sally by her slender waist, Miss Sally holds onto Lance by his wrists, and Lance wiggles like a mealworm, trying to shake Eartha off his legs. It doesn't work.

"Hold tight!" I shout.

The tar pit recedes as the T-Rex continues to sink. The riptide pulls us back down into its gooey depths. I hold tighter. The veins in my eyes pop. They go red. I stretch, struggle and strain. I pull up, I pull up with strength I never knew I had, until I'm there. I'm safe on solid land. I'm out of the tar. Sir Jonas climbs up too, helping pull out Miss Sally, Eartha and Lance.

"No time to waste!" I say. "Everyone into the car! Quickly!"

They all pile in.

"Let's get the hell out of here!" Miss Sally screams.

26

I shove the keys in the ignition and floor it down Route 46. As we speed away, a giant meteor rips through the cloud cover. It slams into the tar pit with a maelstrom of smoke and fire. Black gluey bitumen and liquefied lizard brains rise up behind us in a cataclysmic mushroom cloud of destruction, rendering the last of the hip-hoposaurs extinct.

CHAPTER NINE

I am barreling down the highway, back towards my laboratory.

"I don't understand what happening," Miss Sally weeps. "Dinosaurs? Blacksmiths? Phones that turn into pumpkins? None of this makes any sense!"

"Of course it doesn't," I say. "Overlapping dimensions are coalescing upon us like a cyclone. Every anachronistic impossibility is being deposited into our world at once. The other timelines – every conceivable past, present and future along every conceivable path – are bleeding into our world. The universe is falling apart!"

"So that's what you need the Paraquat Drive for?" asks Eartha.

"The Paradox Drive. Precisely."

"Fairest maiden, you need not shed those tears," Sir Jonas says, wiping a mascara-stained teardrop from Miss Sally's cheek. "I promise that no harm shall come to you."

Lance slaps his hand away.

"Back off, you toolbox!" he says.

Sir Jonas is unfazed. He smiles confidently.

"We have a saying where I come from," the knight goes. "'The weasel can't horde the chicken forever.'"

"Yeah? Well we have a saying where I'm from too," says Lance. "It goes 'Fuck off, cockblocker!'"

"Not to interrupt or nuthin', but is that Abe Lincoln and Hitler makin' out on that bench over there?" Eartha says, pointing out the window. Sure enough, on a nearby park bench, Abraham Lincoln and Adolf Hitler are tongue-kissing passionately.

"Geez, why don't you take a picture?" Hitler lisps. "It'll last longer!"

Then they start giving each other handjobs.

"Oh dear," I mumble to myself. "The incongruities are worsening."

"I don't know about all that," says Eartha. "I mean, Lincoln *is* kinda sexy, don'tcha think?"

CHAPTER TEN

"We're not far now," I say, motioning towards the next traffic light. "It's right up here on the left."

The Earth starts to shake once more as another tsunami of light spills over its surface.

In its wake, the world transforms:

Trees of porkmeat spontaneously spring up from the soil, towering over the downtown office buildings and luxury apartments. Oily bark glistens pale and orange like birthday candles against the city skyline. A few of the trees even sprout fruit – pigs like bananas – bushels of swine hanging by their necks from gnarled bacon-branches. Oinks and snorts and tortured porcine squeals form the soundtrack of the forest as the pignanas are plucked by eight-armed migrant workers, tied together in bundles, and shipped to gourmet butcheries all over the world.

In the glass-domed skull of a 20-foot robot, a caveman is blinked into existence. The caveman, confused by both his sudden awareness and the overly complex nature of modern machinery, smashes the console with a thick, wooden club. "*Ooot ooottt bah,*" the caveman grunts as he accidentally activates the controls obliterating a nearby strip mall with lasers from the robot's eyes. Another robot/caveman shows up and wags its finger at the first robot disapprovingly. The former then challenges the latter to a break-dancing competition. They only get through one round before the dance-off segues into a sensual mechanized lovemaking session. The destruct-o-bots steamroll the surrounding buildings as sparks shoot forth from their grinding metal genitals – the climax of their robo-apocalyptic-murderfuckfest.

And over there it's Jesus! It's Jesus fucking Christ – the Son of God and the Savoir for All Mankind! He's real! And alive! And trying to discreetly buy a porno magazine from a street-side newsstand! A nearby group of paparazzi – who also happen to be talking orangutans, because at this point, why the hell not – are taking pictures of the bewildered Messiah attempting to conceal the sleaze-zine in his ocher-white robe.

"What is this? Who are all you people? Stop following me!" the Son of God yells at them.

And then the light hits us. Once again I am thrust through the entirety of the Universe as all the colors of creation flicker before my eyes like 10,000 TVs playing different channels at once. I die countless times. I'm reborn countless more. By the time it finally passes, my Honda Civic has transformed into a wooden rickshaw being pulled by two very confused Japanese peasants. The peasants scream as the rickshaw careens out of control, swerving back and forth across both lanes of traffic. It's more stress than the poorly constructed 19th century vehicle can handle. A wheel snaps off.

"Kuuuusssooooooo!" the two drivers scream in unison as we wipe out in the middle of the road. I am thrown from the broken, rickety cart and greet the pavement with the flat of my face.

Everything goes black.

CHAPTER ELEVEN

When I come to, I'm covered in shit and piss. But it's not my own shit and piss, which is a relief.

Kind of.

The shit and piss is raining down from oatmeal-colored clouds. I look closer and see the clouds are actually gigantic floating asses lined up cheek to cheek, excreting their watery waste upon us. I puke. It disappears before it hits the ground, then reappears dripping out of one of the assholes overhead, ultimately landing on the back of my head. I stifle the urge to vomit again.

My temples throb. Eartha and Miss Sally lay motionless in the middle of the now-deserted road. Sir Jonas floats facedown in a ditch of thick diarrhea nearby.

I stand and bring my hand to my pounding head. My claws press into my skull. I'm dizzy, bleeding, bruised, but alive. Also I...

...wait a minute...

...my CLAWS?

WHAT THE FUCK!

I look down to see my left arm has mutated into a lizard's leg. It's green and scaly and on the end of each digit are 4-inch claws that are as pointy as pencils and as sharp as swords. I wiggle them to make sure they are mine. Sure enough, the monstrous paw waves back at me.

I'll have to worry about this later. First, I splash down into the ditch and slosh over to Sir Jonas.

"Wake up! Wake up!" I plead, towing his limp body to shore. "Please God don't be dead!"

Five minutes pass. He doesn't draw a breath. Five more minutes pass. It's too late. He's dead. But then, just as I'm about to roll his corpse back into the shit, he suddenly sputters awake, coughing up a turd log the size of a cucumber.

"Sweet Maker," he gasps, "I had the most unusual dream..." Then he sees my lizard arm. He sees Miss Sally beginning to stir. He sees Eartha sitting up, her body swollen to nearly twice its original obese size. "...yeah, it was exactly like this."

He licks his lips then, unsure of what he's tasting.

"Is that...?"

"Yeah," I answer before he can continue. "It would seem that every ounce of shit from the entire span of human history has replaced our atmosphere."

"Well, I'm so glad I got to be *privy* to that," Sir Jonas quips.

The group slowly recollects itself.

"Is everyone okay?" I ask.

"Nice arm," Eartha mumbles through her extra chubbed-up cheeks.

"Nice body," I retort. "What's going on with you, anyway? You're blowing up like a balloon!"

"This...um...this ain't nothin'. Allergies or whatever," she replies. "I have a glandular condition."

"So are we all accounted for?" I ask. "Where's Mr. Schaffer?"

"He's gone," replies Eartha.

"Gone?" I go, "What do you mean 'gone'?"

"Ugh, this is *so* like him," Miss Sally says. "You know, this one time he was supposed to pick me up from work, and he totally ditched me to go play Xbox with his boys."

"The fiend!" Sir Jonas crows, taking her hand into his. "I shant ever 'ditch you,' my dear. I don't even know what an 'Xbox' is!"

"We have to press on," I insist. "I'm sure he'll turn up somewhere."

"I hope so," says Miss Sally. "Because I'm gonna slap him across his sorry-ass face!"

CHAPTER TWELVE

"Well, this certainly isn't going to make things any easier," I say, looking up. We are at the base of a massive mountain. A citadel. An impassable peak on top of which my home humbly sits.

"Was this mountain here before?" asks Miss Sally.

"Yes, Miss Sally," I facetiously reply, "I've always lived at the top of an impossibly tall mountain. I like the fresh air."

"So...is that sarcasm...or, I mean...is the air actually better?"

I roll my eyes and plop down on a rock.

"I think it's time to admit it," I somberly declare. "We have failed."

"Whadaya mean?" asks Eartha.

"Look at me, Eartha. I'm a loser. A broken man. An unrealized genius. I AM THE GREATEST TRAGEDY TO EVER BE BORN! I can't even hold down a job at the local middle school. Why did I think I'd be able to mess around with the space/time continuum? I fucked up, Eartha. I fucked everything up. I mean, look at what we're doing right now. Scrambling around like ants whose hill has been kicked! And for what? To what end? What are we trying to prove? That Fate has to answer to us? That we're smarter than everyone else? That we, above all, are the masters of the tide? This mountain that has spontaneously appeared here before us, it's not just physical. It's symbolic. It's the whole goddamned Universe. We are just...so, so small compared to it all. We might as well just kick back and wait for the next wave of light. Maybe it'll erase us out of existence for good. That's the only end to this sad story; the solace I can see on our ever-darkening horizon."

The rest of the group is looking at me in shock, unsure of what to say next.

"No!" Miss Sally finally exclaims, her face like a sturgeon; a contorted cute little pout.

"Excuse me?" I go.

35

"No!" she repeats. "That's unacceptable! Don't you see, Dr. Dracon? You *do* control the tide. You caused this mess to happen. It wasn't written down in some book somewhere. It wasn't fated. It was *you*. Your influence. *You* changed the world! I'm sure it's not in the way you intended, but nevertheless, you did it, Dr. Dracon. And you're the only one who can fix it. We can't give up. Not now. Not when we're this close!"

"I appreciate the vote of confidence, Miss Sally, but this is one big-friggin'-mountain in front of us and I just don't see how we'll reach the summit in time. That is, unless some sort of gondola lift has somehow magically appeared in your handbag. Has a gondola lift magically appeared in your handbag?"

"Maybe," she lights up.

She sticks her arm elbow-deep into her purse and pulls out a handful of Madagascar hissing cockroaches.

"Nope," she says, "just these terrifying insects."

Eartha wraps her mouth around Miss Sally's fist and slurps, swallowing down the bugs without even bothering to chew. Her cheeks billow out to double what they were a moment ago, and her bulging belly distends even further.

"What ch'all lookin' at, huh? I'm HUNGRY. I ain't ever been so hungry in all my life! I feel like I could juss I dunno...eat the whole damn world!" She scoops up a handful of dirt and throws it down her throat. We're staring at her dumbfounded. "Oh, stop actin' like *this* is the weirdest thing y'all seen all day," she says.

"If only we had access to my stable," Sir Jonas laments. "My team of trusty steeds could conquer this mountain with ease!"

He looks down, defeated, and kicks a small rock across the street, watching as it settles into an abutment of three boulders. The boulders start to quake. They shimmy and shake and rattle and roll. The boulders begin morphing. They grow fur and sprout legs, hooves, snouts and ears. The rocks rise up and neigh because they are no longer rocks at all, but rather three magnificent white horses standing before us. Sir Jonas skips gaily towards the animals.

36

"Vicissitude smile upon us!" he exclaims. "Buttercup? Winifred? Drippybutt? Is that you guys?"

The horses neigh in the affirmative.

"Glorious day! My team is here!"

"Well okay then," I say, reinvigorated as I climb onto Drippybutt's back. "Does anyone want to tell me how to ride this thing?"

CHAPTER THIRTEEN

Eartha appears to be growing exponentially now, and within the hour she's ballooned to nearly 600 pounds. The others are looking at me for some sort of scientific explanation. All I can come up with is that she's somehow *fatassifying*, which I'm almost certain isn't a real thing. Or maybe I just discovered it. Either way, I'll be sure to document my findings once this whole ordeal is over.

Halfway up the mountain and Eartha is now 3,600 pounds. She indiscriminately eats anything that crosses her path. All the strange new fauna that roam these hills – birdrams, chunkminks, brain-squirrel and caterpillows – all the woodland creatures of this strange, new world reduced to nothing but hors d'oeuvres in this blob-woman's unending lunch.

Soon Eartha can't even walk anymore. Arms and legs disappear into a perfectly spherical torso. Just her face, smiling, in the center of a ball of flesh. We attach her to our horses with chains, slowly dragging her 12,000 pound bulk the rest of the way up the mountainside.

Truth be told, I too am experiencing some strange new developments related to my lizard arm. Scales continue to grow, forming along my spine and up my neck. Spreading like ivy. My eyes have begun to take on a yellowish hue and my pupils have contracted into narrow slits. And then there are the uncontrollable homicidal urges I've been feeling as of late, although those might be symptoms of my fatigue and frustration, rather than my sudden reptilian...predicament.

KNIGHTS OF THE WHITE CASTLE

CHAPTER FOURTEEN

Finally, we reach the mountain's summit. A cold wind blows. I can feel my body temperature dropping quickly. I wish I had a heated rock to curl up on. My brand-new tail wraps itself around my torso in a futile attempt at keeping it warm.

There's my small, shitshack-of-a-house, alone on the peak of this cumbrous bluff like a flag left by some long-forgotten explorer. By now the overcast asses have cleared. The moon – the *actual* moon – shines through, illuminating the city rife with turmoil and quantum confusion far below. The dimensional breach in the distance has started to glow once again. Another time wave is building up. We must act quickly, before it's too late!

By this point Eartha has grown to around 12,600,000 pounds and is far too big to fit through my front door. Employing a series of ropes and pulleys, we somehow manage to roll her up to a window instead. Her grotesque 14-inch eyeball peers inside.

"All clear," she says. "Hey, any a' you guys gonna eat this lawn chair?"

Before anyone has a chance to answer, she inhales all of my patio furniture.

We enter the house. My laboratory is in the basement. We pass through the foyer, the hallway, the living room. In the kitchen every appliance instantaneously comes to life. The microwave claps open and closed. The blender wails. Spoon and forks chirp in the counter drawer.

"Dada! Dada!" I can hear them calling out to me.

"Not now fellas," I say. "Daddy has work to do."

Down the stairs, through the laundry room, and we've entered my workspace.

The time machine, in all its complex, technological glory, sits in the center of the room – an overturned refrigerator box, covered in tinfoil and scotch tape, words inscribed in thick, black marker reading 'TIME MUSHEEN' across its upper end. A panoply of wires connects it to a small Texas Instruments graphing calculator on my desk.

"This is it?" asks Eartha, peeking in through the basement window now. "*This is your 'big invention'? It looks like somethin' a kindergar'ner made!*"

I chuckle. "Now, Eartha, I doubt a kindergartener has the intellectual capacity to harness the time-bending properties of your average refrigerator box."

"But dude, I mean, you ain't even spell 'machine' right."

"Yeah? And The Beatles couldn't read sheet music. What's your point?"

I power on the calculator and start punching in numbers. Christmas lights stapled to the device's side flicker to life, casting the room in pallid pink tones.

*Beep*Boop*Bloop*Bleep* the time machine honks and bleats as I maniacally type equation after equation into its central computer. Suddenly an arc of blinding white light flashes forth from the metal hanger on top of the refrigerator box. The house rattles violently as it fills with steam and the time machine hums like an old lawnmower, which makes sense because its motor used to belong to an old lawnmower.

"There we are! It's ready!" I shout to the knight. "Sir Jonas, I bid you make haste! You must get in!"

"I'm afraid I can't let you do that, Mr. Dracon," comes a voice from behind us.

We all turn around. Lance Schatter is standing there holding a machine gun. He is dressed in the traditional royal vestments of feudal England – a surcoat of camel hair, a peacock-feathered belt, a velvet cape of threaded gold, and a crown of precious jewels adorning his stately head. Behind him, a small army of hideously mutated knights stand at attention, armed with machine guns of their own. Every green, grimacing face is attached to a veiny, muscular frame that bulges through their armor like cheese through a cracker hole.

"I see you're admiring my legion of super-mutants. Don't worry, Mr. Dracon," he says, placing his fingers lightly against his temple, "I'm controlling them with my mind. They won't fire unless I..."

Just then, one of the mutant knights accidentally pulls the trigger. *BLAM, BLAM-BLAM, BLAM BLAM,* the machine gun sings before falling awkwardly silent.

"What the fuck, man?" Lance snaps.

"Sorry boss," replies the mutant.

"Okay," Lance says, turning back to face us, "That was a fluke. From here on out they are NOT to fire UNLESS I WILL IT, right?"

He shoots the errant knight a dirty look.

"Lance?" Miss Sally says softly. "Lance, what is this? What are you doing?"

Immediately upon seeing her, his eyes begin to tear up.

"Sally? Is that you? It's been so, so long...." He wipes his eyes and clears his throat. "No. It doesn't matter. It doesn't matter how long it's been. You broke my heart, Sally. You broke it in half. And what is a man with just half a heart? I'll tell you: he's no man at all. I know I might not have been the best boyfriend in the world. I know I was kinda selfish when we were together. But I loved you. That's gotta count for something, don't it? I loved you with everything that I was. But what did that mean to you? Huh? You...you...you left me. You didn't care. You just fucking left me. And for what?" He motions to Sir Jonas. "For him?"

"Lance, what are you talking about? We're not broken up. And there's nothing going on between me and Sir Jonas."

"Not YET, Sally. But there will be." He sighs. "You see, when I fell off the rickshaw back there I was swept away in the color wave. It dragged me backwards. Backwards through time. And I saw everything. All the interchangeable pasts. All the current presents and possible futures. And through it all – through all the various universes that can and do exist – only one thing remained constant: You end up with him, Sally. You'll be his wife."

"Lance...I...I'm...sorry for what I may or may not have done in a different Universe, but this is just crazy!"

"I managed to escape the wave sometime during the 14th century," he continues, ignoring her pleas. "Three-fourths of a millennium ago. Heh...seems like only yesterday."

"King Schaffer!" Sir Jonas booms. "I knew we would finally meet again."

41

"Hello Jonas," says Lance. "You have no idea how long I've waited for this day."

"Nearly 700 years," the brave knight says. His eyes narrow as he grips the hilt of his sword.

"What is the meaning of this?" I finally intercede. "What have you done, Mr. Schaffer?"

"Mr. Dracon," he says to me with a sinister smile, "I always knew you underestimated me. You thought I was a loser. A troublemaker. You never thought I would amount to anything, did you? But when I fell through the wormhole, when I was forced into the past, I rose through the ranks from peasant to king! That's right, Mr. Dracon. The boy you gave straight Cs to is now the king! The King of Hamburg!"

"The *Burger* King!" Sir Jonas sneers.

"I'm afraid that if you send Jonas back to his own time, it may undo everything I've spent the last 700 years achieving. And I can't let you do that."

"Lance, have you lost your mind?" Miss Sally screams.

"Perhaps," the Burger King goes, "being omnipotent tends to do that to a person."

"Did he juss call that fool the 'Burger King'?" a 961,600,000,0000 pound Eartha asks, looking in through the window. "I just got that. *Hahaha*!"

"Now, my friends," Lance warmly whispers, "prepare to die."

The mutant knights raise their guns in unison. Miss Sally closes her eyes. Sir Jonas stands helpless. His mighty sword is no match for their mightier arms.

I gulp. My stomach gurgles, churning with nervous acid and bile. Or perhaps it's just the fast food from before. Or both. I can feel it. Like fire. My intestines contract, bubble and boil. The gas is working its way up through my stomach, past my esophagus...

...and then I burp.

KNIGHTS OF THE WHITE CASTLE

Flames shoot out of my mouth.

I snap my jaw shut. King Schaffer and his knights leap back a step, terrified.

"Holy shit!" Eartha cries. "Homeboy can breathe FIRE!"

I look to the rest of them. Sir Jonas gives me a quick affirmative nod. I nod back.

Pulling deep breaths of air into my increasingly queasy belly, I embrace the nausea, open my mouth and belch with all my might.

BBBBBRRRRAAAAAGGGGGHHHHH!!!!

A cone of pure napalm spews forth, setting Lance and his genetically engineered cohorts aflame.

Burning mutants stumble about the laboratory, blind and helpless. Screaming. Smoking. The smell of barbequed flesh fills the air. Delicious barbequed flesh....

I can't help but feel hunger pangs. I never did get to finish my dinner.

A smoldering knight drags his charred body up the stairs and into the kitchen. He turns on the faucet to douse the flames, but the sentient sink doesn't appreciate being touched that way. Instead it wraps its hose around his wrists and pulls him down into the drain, blood and black entrails spraying in all directions as the unlucky knight sinks into the whirring garbage disposal. Another knight is trampled to death by a stampeding herd of ottomans. One of the walls slides down like the mouth of a ventriloquist's dummy, swallowing several mutants whole. The entire house undulates. The blinds slowly draw themselves closed, and the doors shut and lock. Drywall quivers like it was made of jelly. The entire house is alive...

...and it's got a taste for blood.

Liquefied plaster and aqueous asbestos pour in through the light sockets. The caustic solution sizzles as it dissolves the fetid corpses piled up around the house.

43

"It's stomach acid. We have to hurry," I shout. "Before the house digests us alive!"

I'm back on the calculator, smashing buttons like a madman. The time machine putters and hums. The house-juice is ankle deep now, virulent stomach secretions dissolving my shoes, eating away at my toes like a hundred tiny boy scouts with a hundred tiny pocket knives. I look down to discover a hundred tiny boy scouts doing just that. The pain is intense. Where are their parents? We're so damn close! I *will* fix this.

"It's ready! Sir Jonas, get in!"

The knight peers hesitantly through the doorway cut into the refrigerator box. It glows, foreboding and pink inside. He turns back to me.

"Thank you, Sir Phineus Dracon," he says. "Your bravery will not go untold. And when I speak of you, I will tell the tale of the courageous man who saved the entire Universe on this historic day."

"And to you, good Sir Jonas," I bow. "It's been...well...interesting...I guess..."

The knight then turns to Miss Sally.

"Well, Miss Sally," he says to the girl. "I guess this is goodbye...."

"YOU'RE GODDAMN RIGHT IT IS!"

We spin around to see Lance's shambling corpse, completely cooked yet still somehow clinging to life. A blackened skeleton of a man – melted fat and charred meat dripping from his broiled bones. Only the piercing whites of his eyes remain, ripping through the emptiness of his body and soul like twin supernovas in the darkest galaxies of unknown space.

He lunges towards them. Miss Sally screams as he tackles her. They both fall into Sir Jonas. All three of them stumble back. Back...

...into the time portal. The machine rattles violently. Light so blinding, I cannot see....

"Oh crap," I mutter.

And then the time machine explodes.

EPILOGUE

I step out of my cave.

The purple-green blaze of an alien sun beats down upon me. I yawn, stretch, and begin to flap my wings. The bulk of my body lifts up off the ground. In the air I am free. High above Planet Eartha I soar.

"Hiya, doc," Planet Eartha says, her voice echoing like thunder across the countryside.

"Good morning," I reply into a nearby canyon, which doubles as her ear canal.

"Gettin' to work early, I see?" Her thoughts are the clouds; her words are the wind.

"Always, Eartha. Always."

Many years have passed since the time machine malfunctioned. Since the Universe died. Since it was reborn. Since my grand experiment failed.

Eartha, the dimwitted former fast-food employee's growth finally tapered off somewhere around 13,200,000,000,000,000,000,000,000 pounds. She had eaten and now occupies the entire mass of my former home planet.

Our new home, Planet Eartha, is a very different place.

Here, all things are possible. If you can dream it, it can happen. It *is* happening. It has already been done. I guess, in that way, the world is now a bit better than the place I used to live. Back then, I used to constrict myself; my point of view. In the old Universe, my mind was bound by these puritanical notions of 'physics' and 'reality.' By what I thought *could* and *could not* happen. Looking back now, it was almost quaint. Like a baby. We were all babies then. We were all so innocent. Once the goggles came off and we got to see how complicated and chaotic the Universe *truly* was...

...shit, man.

KNIGHTS OF THE WHITE CASTLE

But I guess there's no turning back now, eh? Time waits for no one. It certainly doesn't wait for me.

Up ahead I see a castle. A White Castle! – towering archaic against the Technicolor dawn. I land on the drawbridge and pound my scaly fist against the gate. A porter peeks his head up over the battlement.

"He's returned!" the terrified porter screams. "The *dragon* has returned!"

The obligatory squad of archers takes its place along the parapet, bows drawn, poised in a perfect tableau. All arrows pointed directly at me. Not that they could do much harm. My skin is like armor. It would take a lot more than a small battalion of mere *men* to hurt me.

The gate slowly grinds open. A magnificent man steps forth to much fanfare, hand in hand with his lovely wife.

"Good morrow, Sir Phineus," he says to me.

"And a good morrow to you, Sir – er – I mean, *King* Jonas." I genuflect on my hind leg. "Good morrow to you as well, Queen Sally."

She bows.

"Still trying to fix the past, I see?" King Jonas says with a light chuckle. "When will you learn? The sun doth surely rise, regardless of the tide. Tomorrow is but a memory, Dragon."

"Indeed, Good King Jonas," I hiss, "but what are we if not stubborn fools, desperate in our attempts to cling to what we believe must be true? I'm so close to fixing all of this, my King. Just the turn of a screw or the tweak of a decimal and I think I might just have it. But, alas, Good King, how my hunger grows! And as you may or may not know, GREAT GENIUS such as mine requires GREAT FUEL to efficiently operate. As such I have come here to humbly beseech you for a bite to eat."

He sighs and looks towards his queen. Miss Sally shrugs. He turns back to me.

"Very well then," King Jonas goes. "I assume you want the usual?"

"Yes, sir. Very good, sir. Thank you, sir," I excitedly yelp.

He claps his hands. The porter runs up.

"Aye, King?"

"Fetch me 47 Hamburgers and a side of French guys."

The porter does as he is told, slaughtering their prisoners from Hamburg, executing their Parisian captives. All to feed me, the Beast, waiting outside their gates.

The bodies are piled up. 47 of them. Brick by brick, just like a pyramid.

King Jonas and Queen Sally disappear back into their White Castle. The drawbridge rises. The archers are at ease.

And I eat.

I chomp on skulls and suck the flesh from bones. I wallow in entrails and splash around gleefully in pools of blood. I let out a roar as I crane my neck to the sky, fire pouring like a flamethrower from both my mouth and nostrils. As much as I still try to fancy myself a man, I cannot deny my true dragon nature.

Back in my cave, back betwixt the stacks of skeletons – all those unlucky, butchered souls foolhardy enough to think they could come to MY HOUSE and slay ME – there sits a broken down refrigerator box, static and inert. Like a piece of furniture. Or maybe it's more like a totem pole. Or perhaps a tombstone. My TIME MUSHEEN – the last remaining vestige of a long-forgotten era. Most people will say that the person who created this machine never existed. But they'd only be partially right. Most people will look upon my efforts and ask, why? Why am I trying so hard to change things? This is the world. This is life. Why can't I just be happy with that?

Why?

Because I still have to look in the mirror every day.

Because I'm the same fucking monster I always was.

And I haven't given up yet.

48

SOMNAMBULANT

a novella by Danger_Slater

TODAY Part 1

When I wake up I'm standing at a bus stop in Paterson, New Jersey with a tan, sober-faced gentleman resting his hand heavily on my shoulder.

"You are doing a great service to the Almighty," he says to me, his broken English lapping at the bearded shores of his crusty lips. His accent choppy like Red Sea waters. His grip tightens, almost into an embrace. "Thanks to the sacrifice you're about to make, the whole world will soon awaken new. Your bravery will not soon be forgotten."

"Um...gee, thanks, dude," I say with a smile, unsure of who he is or how I got here or why I'm wearing this ratty old camelhair trenchcoat on what is undoubtedly the hottest day of the summer.

So now we're just sort of staring at each other. He looks like he might cry. His eyes are black, yet soft, like lava rocks in his skull. The intensity of his obsidian gaze – the respect, admiration, even the *love* he seems to radiate are all making me increasingly uncomfortable, and for a moment I consider telling him the truth: that I'm a sleepwalker. That I just woke up. That I have no idea who he is. That I have no idea what's going on right now. And that I have no control or memory of anything I may have done or said during my somnambulant state.

I want to tell him these things, but I don't. Instead I just return his embrace and reply to his reverence with an affable nod of the head. I've learned over the years that it's usually best to let these situations play themselves out. Just suffer through the awkwardness, smile at the confusion and wait. Then, when I see my window, I duck out with no explanation or fanfare. I just disappear. Like an apparition. An imaginary friend. A dream. I try to avoid having to answer for my behavior. My condition. It's medical. It's beyond my control. But nobody wants to hear that. People tend to react a bit...impulsively when they feel like they've been lied to. I've been punched in the nose more times

49

than I've got fingers and toes. So if I can somehow avoid having *that* happen, yeah, I'm going to avoid it.

Thing is, people don't like being jolted awake from the dream they've come to accept as reality. No good conversation ever began with the words, "I'm not who you think I am..."

Plus, he probably wouldn't believe me anyway. Hardly anyone ever does.

"Can I ask you something?" I go, pushing his hand gently aside. He pulls it back into the folds of his tunic.

"Of course, Dylan! Anything, my friend!" he replies.

"So, um, I don't want you to take this the wrong way, especially since we're such good buddies and all, but...uh...who are you again?"

His smile quickly collapses into a frown. Now I feel guilty. The moment we just shared was rather heartfelt. I shouldn't have let a little thing like cognizance ruin it.

"Now is not the time for games, Dylan." His voice has gone stone. "You have your orders. We are all counting on you."

"Yeah, yeah. Never mind. I was just playing around anyway. You know me...always kidding around and, um, stuff. So yeah, you can chill out there, beard guy. No worries. I got this."

Ya know, whatever 'this' is.

* * *

The Greyhound pulls around the corner, slowly rolling up to the stop. The brakes squeal as it comes to a halt, hissing like a jungle cat as it blows its noxious dog breath in our faces. Passengers begin to board. He motions for me to get on.

"I wish you the best of luck, my friend. In this world and the next." We hug. "And remember, it is imperative that you do *not* deliver the package until you are in the exact center of the tunnel."

"The package in the tunnel?" I clear my throat. "I mean, sure. Package. Tunnel. On it."

"Praise be to Allah!" he proclaims, raising his arms to the sky.

"Uh, yeah bro. If you say so. *Ah-salami-lake-um* or whatever."

He bows respectfully. I bow back and get on the bus.

* * *

I slink down the aisle and take a seat near the back, next to a tough-looking 18-year-old wannabe gangsta wearing two sleeves of assorted black-inked tattoos and about three tons of gaudy platinum-plated jewelry. He sneers at me as I plop down next to him.

"Are you outta yo' fuckin' mind, man?" he asks after giving me a quick once over.

"Huh? Oh, I can find somewhere else to sit," I sputter.

"Nah, son. It's the jacket. What the fuck's up wit' yo' jacket?"

"The jacket?" I say. "Oh right, the jacket I'm wearing. Ha ha. I – uh – I won it. At a church social. It was the grand prize. Yup, my ambrosia salad is to *die* for. I can give you the recipe if you want."

His eyebrow twitches.

"It smells like cat piss," he says.

"It does kind of smell like cat piss, doesn't it?" I say, noticing the smell for the first time myself. "Will you excuse me for a moment?"

I quickly stand and make my way to the lavatory, letting the bathroom door click shut behind me. Why the hell *am* I wearing this stupid jacket anyway? It's a billion-fuggin'-degrees outside and I look like I'm Lord of the Bag Ladies.

Crumpling it in a ball and stuffing it behind the stainless steel bucket Greyhound tries to pass off as a toilet, I turn to the sink and splash some water on my face.

Well, I'm glad that's over. And that's when I see my reflection in the mirror.

My head is wrapped up in blood-soaked gauze. My eye is swollen black and blue. My arms are covered in half-healed lacerations. I'm missing one of my pinky fingers. And I have about six pounds of plastic explosives duct taped to my chest.

I sigh.

It's going to be one of those mornings.

SOMNAMBULANT

When I wake up, I am standing in the center of a plush, red carpet. The scuffs and scars of a dozen designer heels surround me like freckles. Then the click and flash of shutters and camera bulbs and the screams of a thousand hysterical people overtake my senses. For a moment I am lost in the blur of color and noise; I'm nothing but a smear of myself, atomized by the excitement that surrounds me.

And then I blink and things slowly start to come into focus.

I'm in Hollywood. At a movie premier. I'm wearing a clean-pressed, custom-tailored tuxedo and I'm walking hand-in-hand with the film's staring actor, Will Smith.

"Will! Will! Can we get a quick interview?" *Admittance Tinsletown's* Tommy Shrub shouts from off to the side.

I try to run but Will squeezes my hand tighter and drags me over to where Tommy is standing.

***

TOMMY SHRUB: So, Mr. Smith, a lovely night for a premier, don't you think?

WILL SMITH: It is, isn't it? They said rain earlier, but I don't think it's coming. Not that I'd let a little rain *rain* on my parade. Ha ha ha.

TOMMY SHRUB: What the fuck are you talking abou...? Oh, wait! I get it! Ha ha ha ha ha. Because 'rain on my parade' is a common idiom often used to refer to displeasing things other than rain ruining one's good time. And you used it to refer to *actual* rain. Delightful! Ladies and gentlemen at home, that is what we in the entertainment 'biz' refer to as an 'ironic quip.'

ME: [mumbling, confused, groggy] What...what's going on?

TOMMY SHRUB: [ignoring me] So, Mr. Smith, would you mind telling us a bit about the new movie?

WILL SMITH: Well, Tommy, it's an erotic action-comedy called *Cockhand*. In it I play the titular character Cockhand – a somewhat reluctant superhero unable to come to terms with the magnitude of his own power. It's a lot like this other action-comedy I did a few years ago called *Hancock*, except in this new movie both my hands are dicks. Hence the title *Cockhand*. The whole story sorta comes full circle like that.

TOMMY SHRUB: I was lucky enough to get the chance to sit down recently at an advance screening. It's absolute horseshit.

WILL SMITH: Why thank you, Tommy.

TOMMY SHRUB: [motioning towards me] And who is this you're with this evening?

WILL SMITH: This handsome little fuckrag standing next to me is my fiancée, Dylan Spotter.

ME: Fiancée? *Fiancée*?!?! What the hell are you talking about?!

TOMMY SHRUB: Dylan, you're a relative newcomer to Hollywood, aren't you? How's it been treating you so far?

ME: I'm sorry, did Will Smith just say that he and I were engaged?

TOMMY SHRUB: Oh please, Dylan. Don't be so coy. Who is it you're wearing tonight?

ME: Listen, this is a huge misunderstanding. I'm a somnambulist. I just woke up five minutes ago. I don't even know how I got here. I certainly don't recall ever meeting you before, Will – er – Mr. Smith. [starting to weep] I just...I just want to go back home, okay? Please, I beg you, for the love of God, may I leave?

TOMMY SHRUB: Ha ha ha ha ha! Ladies and gentlemen at home, another perfect example of Hollywood's infamous 'ironic quippery.' Although I don't really get this one...but whatever! Dylan, why don't you tell us what it's like sucking the dick of one of the biggest movie stars in the world?

ME: Oh Jesus. This is a nightmare!

SOMNAMBULANT

WILL SMITH: Let me tell you something, Tommy. It's not easy 'coming out' in Hollywood. Between the tabloids and the paparazzi watching your every move, not to mention the incessant calls from my insanely overbearing mother, there's a lot of pressure for me to fit into a certain mold. People expect me to be this big tough guy. Mr. Macho. To be calm and cool and always in control. And I usually am. But then, last month my wife Jada – well, my *ex-wife* now – took me to a performance of *Carmen* at the San Francisco Opera House, and Dylan's unique rendition of *Habanera* literally made me cream my boxer shorts right there on the balcony. I'm tellin' you, Tommy, it was like the Fountain at St. Peter's Square in my drawers that night. Except with cum. I knew right then that Dylan and I were destined to be together. Forever.

ME: Do I get a say in any of this? Are either of you guys listening to me?

TOMMY SHRUB: [ignoring me] I've got to tell you, Mr. Smith, the way you 'came out' was very courageous. Hiring half a dozen skywriters to spell out I <3 PENIS over the skyline of L.A.... You're like the Mahatma Gandhi of gaylords.

WILL SMITH: I'm not afraid to say it, Tommy. In fact, I want to scream it from the rooftops: I'M A BIG, GAY, RICH AND FAMOUS MOVIE STAR! FOR THE FIRST TIME IN MY LIFE, I AM TRULY HAPPY! And if it weren't for my sweet little poopy-muffin Dylan here, I never would've had the strength to admit to the world who I truly am. He's my rock. [kisses me on the cheek, then nibbles my ear] Love you, baby.

ME: [in shock] Holy. Shitballs.

TOMMY SHRUB: You heard it here first, folks. Will Smith. Actor. Philanthropist. Pole-smoker. And the pole he likes to smoke most of all belongs to this random guy Dylan Spotter, right here next to me.

ME: [defeated] Goddamnit.

TOMMY SHRUB: Live from the Red Carpet, this is *Admittance Tinsletown's* Tommy Shrub signing off. Goodnight!

FIVE DAYS AGO

When I wake up, I'm white-knuckled on the wheel of an Italian sports car. I look down. The speedometer reads 200 kph as we careen around the streets and alleyways on the outskirts of Oslo. I'm not sure how fast 200 kph actually is, but I can assure you, should you ever find yourself waking up while driving a foreign car in a foreign city, ANY speed feels fast.

"Step on eet!" the guy in the passenger seat shouts. His thick Norwegian accent spills out of his mouth like a bucket of lutefisk; chunky and slimy and smelling somewhat...off.

Behind us, police sirens wail. Oslo's finest in hot pursuit. I turn left; they turn left. I turn right; they turn right. I speed up; they speed up too. So I do as my passenger says.

I step on *eet*.

Now the guy in the passenger seat is sticking half his body out the window and using a chrome-plated .45 to fire round after round at the pursuing officers.

"You'll never take us alive, coppers!" he shouts, turning back to me. "That is what you American peoples say when you're in shoot-em-gunfights, ja?"

"What is going on?" I ask, narrowly swerving past a *pølse* cart.

"What is going on is we are away running from cops because you are one crazy-ass fucker of mothers, Dylan Spotter! Are you sure you're not devil of dares or a vroom-vroom race car driver?"

I shrug. "I mean, I might've been at one point or another."

"I'm believing not we are getting away with this!" he says. "It's just like a Hollywood action Will Smith movie. *Bad Boys 2,* are we not?"

"Yeah, well, I wouldn't start celebrating just yet," I say, jerking the wheel to the left as we whip around another street corner, kicking dust and gravel into the air. This little old lady who was standing there eats a mouthful of dirt and shakes her angry fist at us.

56

SOMNAMBULANT

"Holy shit," I say, "Did that little old lady just give us the finger?"

"That is humorous, yes?" he replies.

We continue speeding down quaint village streets, the Oslo PD remaining close behind.

"Can I ask you something, man?" I ask.

"Anything, Dylan. You are like brother of mine."

"Now, don't take this the wrong way, but why are we running from the cops?"

"Why? Is this a game on which you play for me?" he says. "We are running from cops because we just stole this..."

He motions to the backseat. I take a quick glance over my shoulder and am greeted by the jaundiced and tortured face of an asexual piece of human macaroni, forever immortalized in his infamous and everlasting final moment of terror. The sanguine sky reflected like hellfire upon orange waters. Alone on the planks of a dilapidated bridge, the man-figure wails. I recognize the painting instantly.

"Is that – is that *The Scream*?!" I go.

"Is one and only."

"We stole *The Scream*???"

"This is news to you?"

"But...but...why?"

"Your jokes are things I am not understanding," he says. "The heisting of the art was your idea. Last night at the Tjuvholmen we had met and were imbibing of alcohol. And talking we were, discussion of life and art and philosophy and global economics. You and I are agreeing on a lot of things and such we are when you turn to said to me, 'Asbjorn, isn't that painting *The Scream* here is Oslo?' to which I am reply, 'Indeed I believe it is,' to which you are then saying, 'We should go stealing that stupid painting and show the world a thing

57

or two. We could be make ourselves rich and powerful. Leaders of a New World Order,' you were saying."

"I'm sure I said a lot of things last night, Asbjorn, but stealing *The Scream*? That's just...insane! Why the hell didn't you stop me?"

"At first I am trying to do just that," he says. "I said, 'this is bad plan you are having because *The Scream* is a very famous working of art and many people will notice when it is now missing.' But you assure me fervently that you have good plan. That we will not be getting caught. So we steal painting. You can be very persuasive, ja?"

"Goddamn," I mumble to myself.

"Things are wrong?" asks Asbjorn.

"Huh? No. No. It's just...I had a rough morning is all."

"Ja? You and I both. Ha ha. So tell me, Dylan, are you – OH SHIT...ELG!"

"Elg? What the hell is an *elg*?"

He points forward. I look. In the road, a wide-eyed moose looks back.

Oh. An elg.

GWARNNNNK!

The mighty beast brays as the front end of the car smashes into it. The entire vehicle flips forward. We're airborne for a moment – sailing over the moose like a moon might sail over an uneasy night's sky – before landing upside down in the center of the road. The car slides across the pavement. Sparks are born; they live and die in the seconds it takes for the asphalt to disintegrate the roof. We scream. Behind us the police sirens scream. The injured moose screams. Even *The Scream* screams. Up ahead there's a thick tree sticking out of the side of the road like a wall of wood. A wall we're rapidly approaching.

"Well Asbjorn, however brief our time together was, it's been nice knowing you," I say.

"Ja. Likewise," he respectfully nods.

SOMNAMBULANT

Our car slams into the tree's solid oaken trunk. The impact knocks me immediately unconscious.

ONE YEAR, SIX MONTHS, THRITEEN DAYS and 9 HOURS AGO

When I wake up I'm lying in a large, comfortable bed in the center of a pastel-peach room. Flower-scented perfumes and stuffed white bears, and the tickle of pink 750 thread count Egyptian cotton sheets on the soles of my feet. The morning sun pours in through an open window. Waves of gold like ocean waters, ebbing and flowing past the waltzing lace curtains. Silent and sensual, a warm breeze blows like a lover's breath on the back of my neck.

Next to me, she sleeps. Her chest rises and falls. Metronomic. Paced. Never in a rush to leave her lungs, and although this may be a song that will remain forever unsung, she exhales perfectly in rhythm as if reciting a poem in her dreams. Blonde hair splayed in all directions across her pink-cased pillow, chaotic and wild. But it's a particular type of chaos. Controlled chaos. Perfect disorder. The type of chaos that only a creature so stunningly beautiful could hope to wrangle. Our noses are only a few inches apart; her angelic face encompassing the whole of my vision.

Slowly, her eyes open. They're blue. Not the stringent blue of Best Buy marquees or the passive blue of suburban swimming pool liners, but a soft, natural blue. Tepid and cerulean – the kind of blue the ocean is jealous of. The kind of blue that gives starfish purpose and causes whales to sing. She opens her eyes, sees me and smiles.

"Hey there, Mr. Sleepyhead," she says, her voice like chamomile.

I smile back before replying, "Um, hey there...you..."

"You were out for so long I thought you might never wake up."

"I'm awake now," I say. "I'm here."

"Good."

She yawns and settles even deeper into the sheets. I'm agape, overwhelmed, hypnotized by the contours of her body. Her cheekbones, her breasts, her elbows, her hips. Like a mountain range her body shapes the landscape of the bed. I imagine myself a miniature man, lost in her topography. Navigating her valleys. Traversing her hills. Exploring her caverns.

SOMNAMBULANT

"What?" she asks.

"Huh?" I dopily respond.

"Why are you looking at me like that?"

"I'm sorry. It's just...you're so beautiful. You're...the most beautiful girl I've ever seen."

She blushes.

"You're like an angel," I say. "Or maybe a dream."

I reach out and touch her face just to make sure she's real. Her skin is velvety. Smooth. Fragile. Like I could melt right into her if only I were to press down with my thumb. A wave of adrenaline surges up my spine. Her skin against my own...I can't explain it exactly. It solidifies something that has been running through me, through my blood, my heart, for as long as I could remember. Something that was indefinable, until just now.

"It's just an illusion, you know," she says, still smiling. Still allowing my finger to run along the silhouette of her face.

"What's an illusion?" I ask.

"Touch," she replies.

"What do you mean?"

"It's physics. Quantum theory. Our bodies can never really *touch* anything," she says, closing her eyes. My fingers find their way to her ear, where they run along the slopes of her helix. "On the molecular level, the electrons that make up your body repel the electrons that make up mine."

She puts her hand on top of mine and squeezes it closer against her cheek.

"That means that no matter how hard you push, the force of that repulsion will always counteract it. Even this bed you lie upon, on an infinitesimally small scale, you're not really lying on it. You're floating an almost immeasurable amount of space above it. You're flying. I'm flying. We all can fly, but we all fly alone."

61

"But how can what you're saying be true? I can feel you on my fingertips. Right now, I'm stroking your cheek."

"You can only feel the force of our atoms pushing away from each other. There's no such thing as *touch*. Only the illusion of what touch might be."

I frown.

"So what does that mean?" I say.

She shrugs.

"I don't exactly know," she says. "I suppose it means we should spend less time trying to hold onto to the things we'll never be able to truly grasp."

"So what do we do?" I say. "How do we go on?"

"Just lie with me," she replies. "Lie with me and let's just enjoy it. This moment. This day. The time we have before we fly away."

And so I do as she says.

I lie there holding her in my arms. Our hearts beating in unison, but our bodies repelling each other on the most invisible of scales. Perhaps it's the Universe's way of keeping us all apart. Reminding us just how vast a millimeter can be. It's scary and sad, if you think about it for too long. The best we can do is to keep pushing, keep fighting. Keep trying to defy it. Right?

I never figured out where I was. She never told me her name. And as I drifted slowly back off to sleep, I knew only one thing to be inexorably true:

That I loved her.

And, one day, I'd find her again.

SOMNAMBULANT

TODAY Part 2

I pull the camel hair coat out from behind the toilet and put it back on. The scent of human piss now mixes with the cat piss smell. I slowly button it up to my neck and lament for a moment the absurdity of my current situation, made all the more absurd by how absurd it's actually not. Waking up to find myself covered in explosives is not really all that uncommon. Not for a somnambulist like me, at least. I mean, if I had a dollar for every time I woke up either strapped to or holding a brick of C4, a block of thermalite, a stick of dynamite, or small ceramic bowl filled with hexamethlene triperoxide diamine, I'd have at least...like...twenty dollars.

(Hey, look, I know twenty dollars isn't exactly a lot of money these days, but c'mon – how often does the average person wake up tethered to a bomb on New Jersey Transit? Once? Maybe twice tops?)

I exit the bathroom.

"Miss me?" I greet the gangsta as I slide back into my seat.

He just rolls his eyes and does his best to continuing ignoring the obviously mentally ill, pee-soaked freak who, quite intrusively, insists on interacting with him.

"Just joking," I mumble.

The bus bumps along Route 3. Past mini golf courses and run-down diners. Past government-subsidized housing units and strip malls. Each storefront does its best to vie for your attention with its pretty colors, beguiling fonts and blinking lights. I've woken up all of this country – all over the world – and I've seen it everywhere. The neon salvation. The neon cancer. The neon promise that everything is going to be okay. Like all you have to do is step onto their sales floor and somehow all your problems will just melt away. Like all you have to do is hand them your cash and you'll finally, finally be safe.

But it's a lie, of course. People like me know – there is no such thing as safety. Only circumstance.

"Excuse me," I say, tapping my new gangsta-homey on the shoulder, "I know this is gonna sound like a weird question, but do you know where this bus is headed?"

"Bro, I don' know you and I don' wanna be involved in whatever it is you're doin'," he replies before pulling the brim of his hat down to block his eyes.

I frown.

"Gee, thanks. You've been a big help."

Out the window I look, reading the signs along the side of the highway. Looking for some indication of where we're going:

HOWARD JOHNSON – $120 A NIGHT

LOWE'S HOME CENTER – NEVER STOP IMPROVING™

WEEHAWKEN/HOBOKEN – LAST EXIT IN NJ

LINCOLN TUNNEL – 1 MILE – KEEP RIGHT

"The Lincoln Tunnel...?"

And then it occurs to me: what the coat, the cryptic message about delivering the 'package,' the explosives strapped to my chest are for.

"Holy shit! I'm supposed to suicide bomb the Lincoln Tunnel!"

SOMNAMBULANT

<u>THREE DAYS AGO</u>

When I wake up, I'm sitting cross-legged on a rattan wicker chair while three buxom-breasted, brick-skinned women fan me with three very large, lizard-colored palm fronds. In front of me are about 60 or so genuflecting aborigines, painted maroon with berries and clay, prostrated in reverence and prayer.

"Br'Khuna, praise thee. Br'Khuna, praise thee. Br'Khuna, praise thee. The Hallowed One is here!" the islanders chant softly in unison.

"Are they – are they worshiping me?" I ask one of the bare-boobied ladies beside me.

She smiles a wide, white-toothed smile and nods affirmatively. "J'es," she says.

"Okay. So...why?" I ask.

"J'es," she replies again, continuing to smile and unflappably nod.

"You don't understand a thing I'm saying, do you?"

"J'es." All tits and teeth she is.

"Hmmm...well in that case – cock balls pussy fart dildo anus barf whore pubes..."

Her smile collapses like a fire-ravaged farmhouse.

"What the hell was that, ya creep?" she says, throwing down her palm frond and storming off.

"Of course," I go.

"Br'Khuna, praise thee. Br'Khuna, praise thee. Br'Khuna, praise thee," the congregation continues to chant.

The grass-roofed structure we're in has no walls, allowing the warm, tropical breeze to blow through without obstruction. The breeze passes through my parishioners' open, extended hands. Blowing through the flames of the surrounding torches. Through my dried out, sand-strewn hair.

On a slightly raised altar behind my driftwood throne, a statue stands. It's a statue of me! A nine-foot tall alabaster statue of me! My eyes half-open seductively. A sheepish smirk across my sultry face like I just said something salacious. My alabaster pants around my alabaster ankles, and I'm holding my alabaster dick while urinating on an alabaster sun. The stream that squirts out of my eggshell-white peehole is fresh, clean drinking water, and some of the tribeswomen are waiting patiently in line to baptize and bless their babies in my holy piss.

"Jesus Christ..." I mumble.

"He proclaims himself to be Jesus Christ!" a man in the front row shouts. "Praise be to the Hallowed One! Praise be to Jesus!"

"Huh? No, no, no – I'm not Jesus. Everybody, please, you can get up off your knees."

The worshipers all stand at the exact same time, continuing to look at me with wide, expectant eyes.

"Um...right," I go, "Sooooooo, how's everybody doing tonight?"

The people in the congregation look to each other quizzically.

"We're all right," one of them shrugs.

"Cool, cool. Glad to hear it," I say. "I see you guys brought the bongos out. Nice touch. Alright...um...well then, I'm happy to see you all came out to bow down and kiss the ground I walk on and stuff. Your booby ladies over here are very nice, too. So, then...um...what do they say? Peace be with you all and ashes to ashes and all that jazz and, I guess, amen, right?"

"O Hallowed One! Hallowed One!" a young boy shouts, running up to me. An older woman tries to grab his arm and hold him back, but he wiggles out of her grasp.

"You can stop with this whole 'Hallowed One' thing, kid. To be perfectly honest with you, I'm not totally sure what the word 'hallowed' even means. Just call me Dylan."

"Dill-an?"

"Sure, close enough."

"Dill-an, what are we to do about the Man from the West?"

"The Man...from...the West..." I say, considering each word.

"Yes – the Man from the West and his assembled troops. Surely, that is why you've been sent to us, is it not?"

"Uh, yeah. Of course that's why I'm here," I lie. "So, about this Man...like, what's his deal or whatever?"

"No one is sure exactly where he comes from. Some say he fell from the Moon. Other claim it is the Devil himself; an incarnation of a nightmare made flesh. He appeared, quite mysteriously, on the previously uninhabited island to the West a dozen or so monsoons ago. Slowly, he has been amassing followers. A small army of devotees, different colors and races they are; zealots from all over the globe. It is only a matter of time before their numbers grow too great and the West Island will no longer be able to sustain them. They will need our land. They will attack. Ever since their arrival, our way of life has been under constant threat. But, alas, this day the tides have turned! The Hallowed One – you – are here to free us from the tyrannical shadow of the West's growing forces!"

"So it's a pretty good thing I showed up then, right?" I say. "Lucky me, eh? 'Cause I hate tyrannical forces too, ya know. They're always, like, so tyrannical and stuff. Listen, Short Round, you got a Fearless Leader or President or Chairman of the Board I can talk to?"

"Chairman of the Board...?" the kid gives me a puzzled look. "Do you mean Chief Hana-Kanuikut?"

"Bingo! That's the guy. Can you take me to him?"

"Very well, Dill-an Christ, follow me."

67

* * *

"So you're supposed to be the Hallowed One? The manifestation of Br'Khuna's holy hand, sent to us by He Who Has No End – the Great Pilot of the Sky? *You're* the one it has been foretold would save our people from the Man from the West?" Chief Hana-Kanuikut eyes me suspiciously. "You seem awfully pale, for a Hallowed One. Like a dolphin belly. Or a cloud."

"Yo, Chief Hana-Montana, or whatever they call you – bro, this whole thing is one big mix-up. I'm not this 'Hallowed One' you guys keep talking about. I can't even hold down a part-time job."

"Oh no, Dill-an, I think it is *you* who is confused."

"Yes! Exactly!" I shout. "I'm not who I think I am!"

To this Chief Hana-Kanuikut replies, "Dill-an, If you truly are who you claim you aren't, you must accept who it is you aren't not to be."

"Um...sure...listen, Chief, not to change the subject or anything, but I gotta ask – what's the deal with the sculpture?"

"Sculpture?"

"The one out there. Of me. Pissing on the sun. First of all, what the fuck? And secondly, there's just no way you made that thing overnight. You'd need a team of UCLA art students working around the clock for a week to pump out a statue that big that fast."

"It's the Prophecy! The Harbinger! It is how we knew you'd come, O Hallowed One. How we knew you would be the one to save us from the Man on the West. The statue washed up on shore a few days ago. We were unsure of what it meant. What the implication was. That is, until you showed up here yesterday, seemingly out of the sea as well."

"Ugh. Don't even get me started on how that happened..."

"The Harbinger shows you relieving yourself upon the sun," the Chief continues. "The sun rises in the East. The West is the opposite of the East. Ergo, you are here to save us. It's not rocket science, Dill-an."

SOMNAMBULANT

"It's not any kind of science."

"Well, considering that ours is a primitive, tribal culture, you can see how we logically made that bizarre series of assumptions, correct?"

"I suppose, if I don't think about it too hard. But Chief, there's still all these questions. I mean, how did it get here? Who made this statue? And how do you speak perfect English? What's next, huh? How many coincidences am I going to be forced to accept?"

"Dylan?" comes a familiar voice from behind me. "Is that being you my own two eyes are seeing?"

"Asbjorn?" I cry in disbelief as my Norwegian art-thieving accomplice steps into the Chief's hut, his indefatigable smile as clean and as wide as the Skagerrak.

"Dylan, I am keep smiling like the Skagerrak over here, which as I'm sure you already know, is very wide strait running along southeast section of my country of home, Norway."

We embrace then, slapping each other's backs in a display of brotherly love.

"Asbjorn! What the hell? How did you get here?"

"I am following the plan, ja?"

"The plan..."

"You are forgetting plan already?"

"No, of course not! I'm just...testing you to see if *you* remember the plan, so...why don't you take me through it one last time – in as much detail as your poor English skills are capable of."

"Very well. When we are hitting tree after crash with the *elg*, you are gotten knocked out for just one second of time before immediately bolting upright and you are saying 'I'm gonna make a swim for it,' you say as you run from Oslo *politiet* toward waterfront. You say 'follow the ocean currents, Asbjorn, and meet me there.' 'Where is there?' I am already asking you, but you have taken off all your clothes by then and are diving in all your nudity into North

69

Sea. So you are mastermind. I do as you are saying. I run. I hijack small flying plane and I follow the current of the water until I am landing airplane here of this island. Just like you are saying before, Dylan. I am following the plan to the exactness."

"This is almost unbelievable," I say.

"*Almost unbelievable* and *impossible* are not quite the same thing," interjects Chief Hana-Kanuikut. "Acceptance is the key to understanding. Stop fighting the ocean. Listen to your own advice, Dill-an, and just go with the currents."

I look to Asbjorn. Then back to the Chief.

"...All right," I say. "So, what is it you think *I* can do about the Man from the West?"

"Hahaha, that's a good boy," laughs the Chief, amicably slapping me on the back, "There will be plenty of time to discuss strategy later. But first things first! The Hallowed One has accepted his fate! A feast and a celebration are in order! Let us imbibe liquors and lie with the big-titted women. Let's go all-out, balls-to-the-wall, slap-yo-grandma buck-ass wild!"

"Slap-yo-grandma? You still haven't explained where or how you people learned English or how that idiom managed to work its way into your vernacular."

"*Hahaha!* This guy's hilarious," the Chief says to Asbjorn while pointing at me. "Where'd you find him?"

"Much like you, he found me," Asbjorn says.

* * *

My tribesmen and I party deep into the night, drinking and dancing and going balls-to-the-wall, slap-yo-grandma buck-ass wild, just as the Chief had instructed. Also, I found out that the term "balls-to-the-wall" is not just a figure of speech here, and the drunken islanders and I spent a good portion of the evening just stumbling around the village, rubbing our nutsacks on various buildings and things. But that's just how this tribe gets down. When they party, they party hard. And when their Hallowed One arrives? They party even harder.

70

SOMNAMBULANT

Their Hallowed One.

...er...

I mean, me.

Thirteen defiled huts and eleven hollowed-out coconuts of island rum later, I'm passed out drunk in a bush outside the home of the biggest-titted woman in the village. Faded away, until tomorrow.

Danger_Slater

When I wake up, all I can smell is fish.

Raw fish! All around me! Everywhere! Overcoming me! *Be*coming me! Raw fish so pungent and foul, it hijacks my senses like a suicide bomber. Even when I try to hold my breath, I can taste it as though I were a fish myself, and it was my own breath that was trapped in my mouth.

I am in some sort of small, squishy room. It's dark. Moist. The walls and floor are soft, wet, undulating, and everything – myself included – is covered in this sort of sticky, gooey, fish vomit-scented slime.

Here's a bit of life advice: if you ever find yourself waking up in a tight, quivering, boogery encasement that stinks overwhelmingly of week-old seafood, the most important thing to remember is not to panic. Remain calm. Try and recall what lead up to this point, all the steps you took before you woke up here. Think about it rationally. Pragmatically. Put it all back together. Piece by piece.

So, where was I yesterday?

In Oslo, Norway.

What was I doing there?

I had met a man named Asbjorn in a bar called the Tjuvholmen, and together we formulated and executed a plan to steal Edvard Munch's famous painting, *The Scream.*

Where did I go to sleep?

Hmmmm...the last thing I seem to remember, we had crashed the car down by the Oslofjord waterfront. I must've been knocked unconscious.

Okay. Good. There we go. So that means logically I must've sleepwalked my way to...um... I'm in the...I'm right by the...uh...I...

SOMNAMBULANT

"I DON'T KNOW WHERE THE FUCK I AM!!!" I scream at the top of my lungs. "HELP ME! FOR THE LOVE OF GOD, CAN SOMEONE PLEASE HELP ME! AARRGGHH!!!"

Piece by piece. Rational. Calm.

The cool, fleshy walls seem to spasm and shake. The fish smell gets fishier. A sound like a bullhorn rings out, a high-pitched resounding howl, echoing at me from all sides. My naked body vibrates down to the marrow, and I can feel it from the tips of my fingers to the pit of my soul. A sound like the call of a massive porpoise or a dolphin or a...

"GGWWOOOAAAGGGHH!"

...a WHALE!

* * *

Three years, twenty-one weeks, and eleven days ago, I woke up one morning to find myself waist-deep in a lobster tank at the Monterey Bay Aquarium. Somehow, in my slumber, I had earned a college degree, landed a job interview, got hired as the head biologist in residence and began my first day of work there. And while I spent a good portion of that peculiar day manually masturbating one very sexually jaded lobster, I did manage to pick up a thing or two – perhaps subconsciously, perhaps through osmosis – about oceanic ecology. Cetacean anatomy, in particular.

Now it's been a while, but if I'm remembering correctly, the creature I'm currently inside of is more than likely a mysticeti, or a baleen whale, as evidenced by the fact that I had not been chewed to bits in the process of ingestion. And judging from the diameter of the stomach area in which I am currently enclosed – roughly the size of a mid-tier sedan – it is highly probable that I have been eaten by a *Balaenoptera musculus*, or a blue whale.

Cool. I'm a genius.

Now...how to escape...

In the Walt Disney version of the Carlo Collodi's classic story *Pinocchio*, after being swallowed by the terrible whale-shark Monstro, Pinocchio and Geppetto escape by building a small fire inside the creature's stomach. This causes the beast to sneeze them out of its blowhole. But that could never happen in real life, right? That's just fairy tale shit. If Walt Disney knew anything about whale anatomy, which I'm assuming he DIDN'T, he would've known that it's next to impossible to get to the blowhole from the stomach. I need to be realistic about this...

Maybe, if I can just fall asleep, I'll get all somnambulant again and somehow sleepwalk my way out of here – just as I'd somehow sleepwalked my way in.

No. No. No. That's waaaaaay too risky. There's no telling what I might do when I'm passed out, and chances are I'd most likely drown or suffocate or...I don't know...have sex with a tuna fish or something, rather than get myself to safety. Also, the puddle of half-digested fish slop around my ankles isn't really the most conducive environment for a powernap.

My best bet is to head downward. Down into the body. Hopefully find an anus or vagina or something I can crawl out of. I take a deep breath of fishfunked air as I part the oozing, sinewy curtains, delving ever deeper into the blue whale's gastrointestinal tract.

* * *

I've only slid a few feet into the monster's murky meat before I bump into this mammoth monolith of a muscle blocking my path like an impassible mountain.

It's the whale's whale-sized heart.

Monstro's heart beats slowly. Melodic. Almost like a drum – and not a measly snare or meager floor tom, either. This whale's heart beats more like an orchestra, an army of timpani resounding throughout the chest chamber of the behemoth beast!

As I duck to walk under the ribs, the palpitations of the giant heart start to box me, Joe Fraiser-style. All left hooks. I'm left with no choice but to box the heart back. Right, right, left, left – I throw punches like wedding guests throw rice. I swing, wanton and wild. I uppercut an artery, heel kick a ventricle and head butt the aorta. The heart beats back – *lub-dub-dub-dub* – refusing to stagger. Refusing to cease. Refusing to relent its arrhythmic attack.

SOMNAMBULANT

I'm dazed, stumbling helplessly backwards into the ropes. Punch-drunk. Bruised. Barely standing. The ropes themselves pulsate. Quiver. I look down. These are not actual ropes. Why would there be a boxing ring in here? This is the chest cavity of a whale. The fibers and tendons caging me in are just a part of the monster's biology, pumping blood in and out of the cumbrous organ. So I turn and grab a fistful of meat. I squeeze a tangle of pulmonary veins, squeeze until my knuckles all crack and my fingers start to cramp and still I squeeze tighter, blocking the normal flow of blood to the whale's thirsty heart. It stutters. Stalls. Stops for a minute. The beast lapses into cardiac arrest. The heart seizes, then falls calm as it attempts to reboot itself. I use the moment of vascular silence to make my hasty, limp-legged escape.

Further down into the whale I slither.

Past the lungs I crawl. Over the liver and through the guts to the lower intestines I go, the corrosive array of stomach juices threatening to dissolve me at any moment.

I move quickly.

I wiggle through the whale's intestinal tubing, using the polyps and villi lining its walls to propel my body forward like a human turd. Working my way down, down, and further down still, I pass through the duodenum. The jejunum. Into the ileum. My tunnel growing ever narrower, tighter, as I descend. And descend. And descend until I finally reach my destination. My escape. My orifice of ever-loving salvation:

The sphincter.

Now all I have to do is pop myself out through the creature's rectum and essentially "birth" myself into the ocean. Then it's a short swim back up to the surface, where I'll resume my day like this horrible morning never happened. Easy peasy, lemon squeezy.

Or at least it should've been if, in my haste to escape, I hadn't overlooked one very important and obvious anatomical detail:

The solid and airtight construction of the blue whale asshole.

It is completely impenetrable. Fuckballs. I should've known! During that afternoon I spent as a marine biologist, a large part of my day was dedicated to coaxing a very prudish beluga into letting me finger fuck her anus. (I'm still not sure what the scientific purpose of all this quasi-bestiality was, but both the lobster and the beluga whale went to sleep that night very happy. In the end, that's the important thing, right?) The one thing I took away from that day is that these animals are not letting anyone up their poop chutes unless they *want* you up it. I mean, these bungholes are built to withstand the crushing pressure of the ocean's depths. Unless this blue whale wants to let me out, my feeble body doesn't stand a chance of poking one teeny tiny pinky through its hermetically sealed rectum, let alone my entire bulky body.

The air is getting thinner. The sphincter is constricting tighter. The walls are closing in around me. I suppose I'll just have to resign myself to a slow death by suffocation, here in this blue whale's lower colon.

Sigh...

I always knew it would end like this.

* * *

But then, just as quickly as I'd accepted this horrible fate, an idea suddenly sprang into my head. One that would surely work, given I didn't run out of oxygen and asphyxiate first.

Maybe – just *maybe* – if I could somehow get the whale to fall asleep, its butthole would relax enough for me to punch my way out.

So I do what my mother used to do when I couldn't fall asleep. Back before the...incident...18 years ago. Back before she disowned me. Back before my somnambulance dominated my life. Back before I destroyed hers. Back when I was just a little boy:

I start to sing.

I start out with a soothing lullaby. *Twinkle, Twinkle, Little Star.* I belt it out as loud as I can. Straining my vocal chords until my throat is raw. I hit notes I hadn't thought my body was capable of – notes I'd never even dreamed of reaching when I woke up at that opera last month. I hit notes previously unheard before, singing like my life depended on it because, in fact, my life did depend on it – a difficult task made all the more difficult in the airless tomb of this monster's butt. But I don't stop. I keep singing. I push myself

SOMNAMBULANT

through the pain because this is it, my only chance. I traverse pitches and octaves like the vocal equivalent of a cross-country skier. I glide through melodies like the notes were nothing but white powder. Moving on to a stirring rendition of *Rock-a-Bye Baby*, I could sense the whale growing tired. Seizing my chance, I quickly segued into the next song in my repertoire, the emotionally charged Irish folk ballad *Danny Boy*, aptly changing the lyrics to be more Cetacean-centric:

Oh Danny whale,
The whales, the whales are wailing.
From whale to whale
And down the mountain whale...

I can hear the whale cooing softly now, and as it floats off to sleep I can feel the walls of its rectum gradually losing tension. The mucus stops secreting. The polyps stop pulsating. The great sea beast falls into a peaceful slumber and I immediately start fisting its anus from the inside, but still to no avail. Even with the whale out cold, its butthole is still sealed up tighter than a jar of pickles.

It's hopeless.

But then I hear a rumble. At first it's like a low growl. Like a distant tractor. An airplane buzzing overhead. A slight breeze begins to blow, lightly at first, but getting windier and windier as the seconds pass. Hot, sulfurous gas emanates from somewhere deep inside the creature's guts, stinging my eyes like mosquito bites. There are chunks of feces floating in the air all around me now, like poo flakes dancing the fandango to the songs I'd just sung.

The rumble gets louder. The air blows hotter. Oh Jesus, please God, no. I know where this is heading. And it's going to be bad. The wind kicks up to hurricane speeds and then suddenly – KA-POW!!! – I explode out of the whale's asshole, suspended in the center of a noxious fart cloud.

Into the waters I am cast, miles beneath the surface of the sea. Too deep to swim to safety, there is only the unflinching, uncaring ocean – whether I live or die as inconsequential as each drop making up its mass. But the gas bubble born from the blue whale's bottom proves to be equal parts disgusting and life saving. It protects me from drowning to death in the endless blue sea as the fart floats upward. Upward. And upward I go, until finally my head breaches

77

the water's surface in the harsh light of the midday sun, swallowing great gulps of fresh, clean air as if they were the last I'd ever breathe.

I did it! I am alive!

And up ahead I can see – not even 200 yards off – a fortuitous landmass abutting against the water. A magnificent, virgin beach stretches across its pristine shore, white sands and palm trees beckoning to me. And so I swim. I swim and swim with everything I can swim with. My arms, my legs, even my dick all working in unison to cut through the water, until that beautiful moment when I finally crawl onto its golden shore, dragging my bruised and battered, whale-shit-caked body onto the sand. Beaten. Soiled. Exhausted.

Alive.

I lie there motionless on the beach as two aboriginal men appear from some nearby brush, cautiously approaching me. As they draw nearer, the smaller one's face lights up.

"Is that him, Chief Hana-Kanuikut?" the man asks.

With every ounce of energy left in me, I raise my arm and give them the thumbs up.

"I believe it is," the Chief replies, smirking slightly. "The Hallowed One has arrived."

Then I promptly pass the fuck out.

SOMNAMBULANT

<u>18 YEARS AGO</u>

When I wake up, I'm...I'm...

"Dylan?" a soft voice asks. "Dylan, Can you hear me?" Burnt coffee and stale cigarettes float upon his acerbic breath. Like sour milk and thrift store sofas. Dirty old man smell.

"*Ugggh, uhh,*" is all I can groggily groan.

"No, he's still out of it. Nurse?"

"Yes, doctor?"

"Up his dosage of clonazepam to 4 mg and administer 15 mgs of zolpidem. And get me another blood read, just to be safe. We're not trying to put him down, just let him rest a bit."

"Yes, doctor. Right away," the nurse replies.

"Is he – asleep now?" a more familiar female voice asks. It's a voice I recognize instantly.

The voice of my mother.

"Not quite, Mrs. Spotter," the doctor says to her, "What we're attempting to do here is help induce slumber, though technically, the state he'll be in will be more akin to a coma than what you would call 'natural sleep.' Your son's EEG results have shown extraordinarily elevated brain activity between the delta and REM phases of the sleep cycle. Couple that with a severe malfunction of the automatic muscle paralysis that usually accompanies REM sleep, and you have the most extreme case of somnambulance I've ever seen. It's quite incredible, really."

"You might as well be barking like a dog, doc," my mother says, "because none of what you just said made any sense to me."

"Mrs. Spotter, the most important thing you have to understand is that your son's condition is out of his control. It is not his fault."

79

"So what are you implying, doctor?" she raises her voice. "You saying this is somehow *my* fault?"

"Heaven's no, Mrs. Spotter! Though sleepwalking may be an inherited trait, there are plenty of external and unique biological factors that could contribute to your son's peculiar...circumstances. The truth is, we're not exactly sure why or what causes somnambulance. The brain is a complicated organ. So much of what it's capable of is still a mystery."

"If he inherited this anywhere, it would'a been through his father, I'll tell ya that much."

"Now Mrs. Spotter, this isn't about pointing fingers or passing the blame. This is about your son getting better. About him leading a full and normal life..."

"A full and normal life? A FULL AND NORMAL LIFE?!?" she cries. "What am I supposed to know about a full and normal life now???"

She's upset. I would be too, if I were her. My poor, beleaguered mother. It must be a nightmare to have a son like me. So against the haze I fight. I fight my way up the river. I fight until my eyes finally open – just a sliver – and I can see where I am.

White ceiling. White walls. White coats. White hands. A hospital room. Everything white. Safe and sterile.

My mother stands next to the doctor. Tears run down her face. She looks tired – huge bags under her eyes like tidal pools of black water with no sieve to drain from. Like she hasn't had any sleep in days. Like she's never had any sleep. Where her arms used to be there are just two little stumps, two fractions of two arms, wrapped up in white bandages. Healing.

Where are my mother's arms? What is going on here? What sick son of a bitch could commit such a horrid act against my dear sweet mom, the woman whom birthed me and brought me into this world? The woman whom cared for me when I was sick and caressed me when I was afraid? Who used to sing lullabies to help carry me off to sleep? The woman whose loving embrace always made me feel like nothing could ever go wrong? Whose loving embrace I'd never feel again?

SOMNAMBULANT

And then it hits me. Why she's so upset – the full implication of my condition. I know who chopped off my mama's arms.

It was me.

She's pounding on the doctor's chest with the stumps now. Hitting him, hitting him. And he doesn't even blink. He just stands there. Clinical. A statue. She hits him again and again until, under all that bandaging, her wounds open up. And now that white wrapping is turning red. And she's crying and crying and crying and her bloody arm stumps hit the doctor and blood splatters onto his coat in chaotic starfish patterns of crimson gore. And then, after a while, she's all worn out. And she stops hitting him. And her tears run dry. And she's staring off into space, completely drained of both passion and soul.

"Some of us'll never get the chance at a full and normal life now," she says, her voice just above a whisper. Raspy and raw. "Some of us are victims of circumstance. Trapped forever in our own skin. Doomed to be ourselves."

"Mrs. Spotter, please..."

The nurse reenters the room and gives me a shot of something in my arm. I can feel the drugs coursing through my body. Like a fire in my veins, but not the devastating kind. Not the kind that destroys Chicago. A soft fire flows through me. A campfire. No, it doesn't ravage and destroy. It merely ameliorates – warm and loving. This fire like the last hug I'll ever receive.

"There's no end to this tragedy, doctor." My mom looks at me as my eyes grow heavy and close. "The best we can do is let the little monster dream."

THREE WEEKS, FIVE DAYS AGO

Hidden Hills, California

Will Smith's family home

The following events take place six days <u>after</u> my performance of Carmen *at the San Francisco Opera House and two weeks, five days <u>before</u> the interview with* Admittance Tinseltown *at the premier of* Cockhand.

"No, no, no you fucking idiots! How many times do I have to explain it to you? His eyebrows are lower! His nose isn't so bulbous! And there's a small goddamn dimple in the center of his goddamn chin! What you've done here? This is pure garbage. A crime against both decorum and good taste. It's an abomination!" Will Smith screams, pointing at a 9-foot-tall statue of me pissing on the sun.

"And the penis? You call *that* a penis? In my head I imagine it MUCH larger than that! I'm talking Louisville Slugger over here, not that little...bendy straw you've sculpted!"

"But, Mr. Smith, sir," one of the art students protests, "we've been sculpting non-stop for two whole days based solely off the shoddy description you provided. You've barely fed us. I haven't slept since I got here. And I'm pretty sure I have mono. We're doing the best we can."

"The best you can? The best you can?! Do you have any idea how powerful I am in this town? I AM HOLLYWOOD, BABY!!! Now listen up, you ungrateful twits, I wasn't born with a silver spoon up my ass like you over-privileged little shits were. Mommy and daddy didn't pay for me to go to 'art school' to pursue my dream of becoming a 'liberal heathen' or a 'pretentious hipster douche' or whatever it is you're majoring in. No, in West Philadelphia I was born and raised, okay? On a playground is where I spent most of my days. And you know what they did on that playground? They popped fools for flappin' their lips out of place. You got that, Caleb or Walker or F. Scott

SOMNAMBULANT

Fitzholden Caulfield or whatever trendy yuppie name was popular the week you were born? *I'll* tell *you* the best you can do!"

"Will? Will, where are you?" Will Smith's movie star wife, Jada Pinkett, says as she comes down the stairs.

"Over here dear. Just telling these quote/unquote 'artists' how to do their fucking job," Will Smith says, shooting the students a menacing look.

"Will, baby," she coos. "I'm beginning to worry about you..."

"Jada, honey, there's nothing to worry about," he says. "Everything is fine."

"I know you keep saying that, Will, but your career choices as of late have been a bit...what I mean to say is *Hitch* I can forgive you for, but this new statue project you've been working on is just...it's sort of crazy."

"What's so crazy about it, Jada?"

"I mean, why are you even making it? For what purpose? Who is this guy?"

"Do you remember the opera we saw last week?"

"Wait a second, is this that guy who sang the *Habanera* aria? Will, that was the most pathetic display of opera I have ever seen. His chromatic scales were all fucked up. It sounded like a dog giving birth to a cat! It was horrible."

"Jesus Christ, Jada, it's not always about the skill of the performance. It's about the *heart* of the performer. I mean, *Demon Knight* sucked nards but I never blamed you for that. And do you know why?"

"Why, Will?"

"Because you were young, talented, and you *wanted* it. The script you were workin' with might've blown hyena dick, but your performance in it was Solid As A Rock™ (Sorry, Jada – General Motors pays me to work that phrase into casual conversation a few times a day). Anyway, I saw that same spark in that young man singing his heart out on stage last week. It just...it changed me, Jada. Watching him sing changed who I am inside."

83

"I don't want this to come across as small-minded or anything, Will, but your sudden obsession with the alabaster penis on this statue is...well, baby, it's sort of...gay."

"What's gay about wanting to touch and be touched by this strange man's penis?"

Jada's perplexed and choleric face suddenly loses it angry scowl as the implications of her husband's recent behavior coalesce in her mind.

"Oh my God!" she exclaims. "It's all making sense now..."

"What?" goes Will.

"The Men's Health magazines stacked up in the bathroom. Your all banana and cucumber diet. Agreeing to star in *Cockhand*, the gay-porn version of your movie *Hancock*. Will...are you a homosexual?"

"Jesus, Jada – can't a famous A-list celebrity just want to lay down naked next to a stranger of the same gender in a bed until the sun and the stars and the moons in the sky all die and we are drawn together into the singularity unto which the Universe will eventually collapse and our atoms are forever entwined – just he and I together as one until the end of time itself? How is that homosexual?"

Jada stands there dumbfounded for a moment before calmly addressing her husband.

"Will, I want a divorce."

"Is that how it's gonna be, J? That's how you're gonna do me? Well, fine! Go on then! Get the hell outta here! Who needs you anyway? All I need is my money and mansions and these art students making this statue for me, and to figure out the identity of this intriguing male specimen!"

Jada storms off in tears. Will turns back to the sculptors.

"What the fuck are you fuckers looking at, huh?"

"Nothing, Mr. Smith," one of them replies.

"That's right nothing. Now get rid of this piece-of-shit statue and start over!"

"Get rid of it? Mr. Smith, it's 9 feet tall and weighs 3 tons. What do you expect us to do with it?"

"I don't give a shit. Cast it off into the sea! Get it out of my sight and start over. *Now*, minions, or you'll get no bread and water!"

"Yes sir, Mr. Smith, sir. I'll have it dumped into the Pacific straightaway!"

Danger_Slater

TWO DAYS AGO

When I wake up I'm 40,000 feet above the Earth's surface, plummeting rapidly towards it.

Above me, the steady hum of a single-engine airplane fades like radio static as the frigid air of the stratosphere fills my ears with its whispery roar. Below me, the ocean – blue, open ocean sprawling out in all directions until it swallows the horizon and consumes the azimuth. An ocean refusing to obey its own boundaries. An ocean eternal. An ocean without end.

Like the sky beneath the sky.

And in the center of all that water, surrounded by sapphire and cradled in the cobalt sea, there sits the small green island towards which I am rapidly falling.

For someone who isn't me – someone who isn't accustomed to waking up under such dire and life-threatening circumstances, someone who's never been roused from a peaceful night's slumber in the midst of an epic five mile freefall – this sort of situation might illicit a tinge of panic, if not pants-shitting terror. But not I. Quite banally, in fact, I give the ripcord on my parachute a casual tug and wait to be gently floated to the ground.

Of course, when I pull the ripcord and out comes Edvard Munch's 1910 version of *The Scream* instead, I cannot help but find myself a little...distraught.

The painting seems to float there, just above me, and for a brief moment our expressions match exactly – perfect mirrors of each other. Faces contorted. Mouths agape. The agony of existence painted upon our worried brows. The world that surrounds me is chaos; as convoluted and unstable as the blend of swirling reds, oranges, and blues that twist around the macaroni man's twisted visage. The primal scream that passes through all of nature – that passes through all of me – that encompasses suns and moons and galaxies and stars – the primal scream that manages to finally find a home in my vocal chords before erupting out of my body in a blood-curdling wail. Proof that I suffer. Proof that I exist. The painting and I? We're both stuck in our own particular canvases. We're stuck being us. And no matter how much I kick and curse and fight and cry, I'll never be able to change all the hues and brushstrokes I've come to define myself by.

All around me other parachutes start to open, one after another. *Pop! Pop! Pop!* Aborigines like dandelion seeds populate the sky. My people. My followers. My paratroopers. Floating safely towards the island below. Gradually, all the pieces of this fractured morning slide together like one of those cheap, plastic slidey puzzles that are a real pain in the ass to solve: We must be invading the neighboring island. We must be attacking the Man from the West. This is a military offensive! Above? That's got to be Asbjorn's plane that we leapt from. This must be some sort of black-ops maneuver. And although I have no idea how we got here or what had transpired since I passed out drunk at the rub-your-balls-on-the-wall party, I'm 100% *sure* that all of this was somehow my idea.

Chief Hana-Kanuikut is to my left, falling alongside me. He looks over and gives me a thumbs-up. I swim through the air until I'm right up next to him.

"I don't have a parachute!" I yell into his ear.

"You don't have a pair of shoes?" he yells back.

"Parachute!"

"Pear of soup?"

"Parachute!!!"

"Oh! Okay, okay – calm down, O Hallowed One. I heard you that time," he says with a big smile, reaching behind his back to produce a *parrot suit.*

"Why do you have a parro...you know what, never mind."

Look, it's not like I'm in any position to be hypercritical here. I don't have much time. So I snatch that parrot suit out of his hands and climb into it as quickly as if it were my own skin I'd somehow fallen out of. And then I do what any levelheaded person would do in my situation:

I flap my goddamned arms like hell and hope for the best!

My plushy red-feathered wings fight hard against the wind. Against gravity itself. I even squawk and request a cracker, hoping to somehow channel my inner avian and make like Icarus for the sun. But it's useless. The island is coming up quick.

Oh man. This is going to hurt.

I crash into the thick jungle canopy, branches tearing at my parrot suit, plucking out my feathers as I tumble through the gnarled mess of vinery. I strike my head against the trunk of a mighty palm, poking out through the jungle cover like a middle finger. My brains explode out the side of my skull as the tree's ribbed surface shaves skin and bone off my head like the rind off an orange.

I hit the ground with a thunderous thud and everything goes black.

SOMNAMBULANT

YESTERDAY

When I wake up, I'm strapped to a wooden table in a dimly lit, mud-walled room. My arms and legs are bound with fraying, knotted twine. An unfrosted incandescent bulb hangs from the ceiling by a threadbare wire. The air in the room is cool and moist, like I'm underground, perhaps in some sort of bunker or dungeon.

I struggle to free myself, but the ropes are thick and tied tight. It's no use.

I'm trapped.

"That was quite a feat back there, O Hallowed One," says a familiar voice to my left. I turn to see Chief Hana-Kanuikut next to me, strapped to a second wooden table. "When you hit that tree I thought you were done for. Your brains were leaking out all over the place! It was nasty, dude. If I were a betting man, I'da said that was the end of you. But, shit, Hallowed One, you proved yourself once again. I've never seen a guy perform open-skull neurosurgery on *himself* before! It was breathtaking, really. And how you used that pile of cockatoo feces to help seal the wound...who'da thought a rotten glob of bird shit could have such restorative properties? If there was even the slightest chance of us surviving our current predicament – which there isn't – you probably woulda made the cover of every medical journal from here to Mars."

"Cockatoo feces?"

I tilt my neck up and sniff. A white glob of half-dried bird crap falls out of my head wound and into my mouth. I shriek.

"That's not going to do much good now," Chief Hana-Kanuikut says. "We've already been captured. The Man from the West is not known for his mercy. If we're lucky, we'll only be beheaded. If we're unlucky, we will be crucified and systematically disemboweled while our genitals are ground between two large rocks. Buzzards will eat our mutilated cocks in front of our eyes as we slowly fade into oblivion. Most likely, we're about to suffer horrendous and painful deaths. But such is the destiny of a martyr and a prophet. And I want to thank you personally, Dill-an Spotter Christ, for leading us to our ultimate salvation."

"Chief, I'm telling you again, I'm not who you think I am. I'm not your prophet or messenger from Br'Khuna or whatever you call your god. There was nothing divine about us meeting. I'm just a regular dude who woke up in the wrong place at the wrong time."

"I know you keep saying that, but the Harbinger – the statue of you – it appeared on our shores only days before your arrival. This moment has been foretold. As were the moments before it and the moments to come. As everything is foretold, however infinite the possibilities. This is not mere chance, as you so adamantly proclaim. This is not misfortune. The universe would never make such a mistake."

"It is chance, Chief. All of it."

"You don't know what you're talking about, Dill-an! There is no such thing as luck. There is only what is happening. Here. In the present. And if this is not the way things were *meant* to be, then answer me this: why are they exactly this way? If other outcomes are indeed possible, then why have they not come to pass? You cannot argue with what your own eyes see. You must accept it. Your role in all of this, O Hallowed One..."

"Yes, O Hallowed One," a sarcastic Middle Eastern voice suddenly interrupts, "you *must* accept your role..." I strain my neck up, getting another mouthful of bird poop as a white-robed, white-turbaned figure steps out of the shadows and into the light.

"Osama Bin-Laden?!" I exclaim. "What the fuck is going on? You're – you're supposed to be dead, you terrorist sonofabitch! I saw it on the news and everything. Seal Team Six, or whatever. They made that *Zero Dark Thirty* movie about it and everything."

"You think a bunch of *seals* can stop me?" Bin-Laden sneers through his smirking, bearded lips. "Nigga, please. Seals, dolphins, killer whales – send every animal you've got at SeaWorld my way. I'll take 'em *all* on! Now ask yourself this question: Do I look dead to you, bitch?"

"This guy, always calling people 'bitch,'" another voice suddenly cuts in. "With you, it's always 'bitch bitch bitch.' You really need to stop listening to so much of that American gangsta rap music, Binny. Or at least listen to more wholesome rappers, like Will Smith or something..."

SOMNAMBULANT

Osama turns to his right. Sewn onto his shoulder is the reanimated head of Saddam Hussein.

"Yeah, or listen to me," a third voice interrupts. "I am great rapper, too! Greater than that clown-penis, Psy. I am greatest rapper in whole world says every magazine ever made ever!" Sewn onto Bin-Laden's other shoulder is the head of Kim Jong-il. "We all know I am Supreme Leader of this body so we do as I command."

"Shut up, Kim," says Bin-Laden. "You only control the left arm. That's only, like, 1/8th of our body's total mass."

"Of course, and your ego accounts for 95% of our personality," Saddam Hussein mutters to himself.

"I may only control the left arm, but we all know that left arm is best arm. Like right now, your right arm is thinking 'Oh why am I such a dumb and inferior arm?' I'll tell you why – it's because of things like this: BOMBS AWAY!" shouts Kim Jong-il as he uses his left hand to poke Osama Bin-Laden and Saddam Hussein in the eyes.

"Gah! Knock it off, Kimbo. Can't you see we're trying to intimidate these prisoners here?" Saddam Hussein scolds him, using Bin-Laden's right hand to slap Kim Jong-il in the face. The North Korean dictator quickly ducks his head out of the way, and Hussein accidentally slaps Bin-Laden instead.

A frustrated Bin-Laden leaps into the air and executes a perfect splits, kicking the other two terrorist leaders in their respective heads.

"Jeez Louise with a side of Swiss cheese, you guys are super annoying," he says. "Can we get back to the task at hand here? These captives aren't gonna torture themselves."

"I'm so damn confused," I say. "All three of you are supposed to be dead. What are you doing here?"

"This guy won't quit with the dead stuff," says Saddam. "Just let it go, man."

"You Americans and your media...you wouldn't know the truth if it were a three-headed Superterrorist about to torture you, which, coincidentally, it is! You hide behind your Hollywood movies and gasoline SUVs and all of your

91

Miley Cyrus sideboobs and your genetically modified silos filled with giant corn. Or is that genetically modified corn in giant silos? Whatever. You think you're so above everyone else in the world. Like we're all here to serve only you and your interests. Well, while you people were busy patting yourselves on the back for pissing all over the planet, we – the Terrorist Three – we've been busy reviving ourselves and genetically manipulating our DNA and shit."

"Yes," adds Kim Jung-il, "we are now Ultimate American Ass-Kicking Machine of Doom!"

"Kimsama Bin-Jungsein," Chief Hana-Kanuikut begins, "you have bitten off more than you can chew this time..."

"I don't know about that," says Saddam Hussein. "We do have three mouths...we can chew a lot!"

"This guy next to me, Dill-an Spotter, he is the Hallowed One. Champion. Savior! Chosen by Br'Khuna Himself. He will not let you take over our island and enslave our people. He will stop your plans of total world domination. Isn't that right, Dill-an?"

"Um...I mean...I don't really know...that's a lot of responsibility you're puttin' on me..."

"What? This guy? This guy is gonna stop us?" Bin-Laden laughs. "Oh man. That's funny. Look at how skinny he is. This guy couldn't even stop a fart."

"Hey, I'm nervous," I say. "And they were silent. I didn't know you could smell 'em."

"Smell 'em? Bitch, I can *taste* them."

"Blah blah blah. Can we start torturing these fools now?" Saddam whines. "All this comic book villain pontificating is making me hungry and I got a sweet meatball sandwich waiting for me in the break room."

"Agreed. I got a sweet meatball sandwich too," says Jung-il. "Except mine's even better than his. It's best sandwich in history of Universe."

"All right, so what do you guys say?" asks Bin-Laden. "We get a good hour of torturing in before lunch?"

"Sounds good," nods Hussein.

"Where do we start?" Bin-Laden asks. "Hands, feet, or genitals?"

"Genitals!" Kim Jung-il enthusiastically shouts.

"Of course *you'd* want to start there," Saddam Hussein chuckles. "It's not torture if you use your mouth, Kimbo."

"Shut up, Saddam!"

"Okay," says Bin-Laden, picking up a large, chrome-plated bone saw. He walks over to me and puts the blade to my pinky finger.

"Say cheese," he says, smiling as he presses its serrated blade against my flesh.

It's all just too much.

And I faint.

Danger_Slater

<u>TODAY Part 3</u>

The bus enters the Lincoln Tunnel like a pickle into a concrete esophagus. The daylight shrinks into a single tiny dot in the rearview mirror, and up ahead the lights of Port Authority have yet to be seen. Above us the Hudson River sits, her fat ass resting upon the tunnel walls with all the weight of the ocean. The sounds of traffic echo off the porcelain-tiled bulwark, bouncing around until it's rendered tinny and hollow. Echoes of echoes. The ghosts of sounds. And the tunnel's evenly spaced neon-industrial lighting tract casts us in an anemic orange. These are colors opposite of the natural sun. This light brings no joy. No respite. No amelioration. Instead, it sucks it up like a photophilic sponge. This is suffocating light. Claustrophobic light.

This is the last light I might ever see.

I clutch my coat tighter around my neck, turning to the gangsta next to me.

"*Brrrrr!*" I say, "Cold in here, eh?"

He shakes his head, his face full of contempt. And I can understand that. If I wasn't me, I would wonder what my deal was too. Shit, I *am* me and I'm *still* wondering that.

"Why don' you juss take it off, huh?" he finally says to me.

"Excuse me?"

"That stupid fuckin' coat you're refusin' to remove. It's 120 degrees up in here, probably the hottest day ever. You're literally *drippin'* sweat all ova me. It's fuckin' disgustin,' man!"

"Am I? Oh, I see that now...gross, right? I'm sorry. Unfortunately, though, the coat has to stay on,"

"What you mean 'hasta' stay on?"

"It's just...I have a rare skin condition."

94

He raises a skeptical eyebrow. "And what kinda 'condition' would that be, huh?"

"I...um...I have no skin?" I unconvincingly lie.

"Look, muthafucka," he goes, "I'm getting' real tired a' your shit."

"You have no idea how much I agree with that statement."

"Why don' you take it off?" he threateningly says, pulling a knife on me, holding it low where only I can see it.

"Please, man..." I beg him. "You're about to make this morning *soooo* much worse."

"I said, take it off," his voice cold and flat, "or me and you are gonna have a problem."

I sigh and slowly slip the coat off, exposing the explosives. The gangsta's eyes go wide with fear and his mouth falls open in shock.

"The fuck is tha...oh, shit! Bomb!" he screams. "BOMB!!!"

I hold my hands up in a half-hearted attempt to calm him down, but I already know it's way too late. Everyone on the bus is craning their necks to see what's going on. There I stand – waving my arms in the air like a psychopath, strapped to my chin in plastic explosives.

"Please, everyone, just relax," I plead, standing up on my seat. The gangsta beside me now cowers in the wet spot forming on the front of his jeans. "'DisfuckedupDisfuckedupDisfuckedup," he whimpers to himself. Women squeeze their babies tight. Children sob. Men covertly text message their wives at home – 'HONEY I LUV U <3' – certain that this will be their last tweet ever twitten.

"This is just a huge misunderstanding," I say. "You see, I'm a somnambulist..."

"Somnambulist?!?" someone shouts from up front. "He's speaking Farsi. Terrorist! TERRORIST!!!"

The bus erupts into total chaos. Passengers clamber over the backs of seats, others clawing their way down the aisle. Knees and punches and elbows are thrown. There's screaming and crying and praying and yelling and fighting and barking and begging for mercy.

"No," I say, "you people need to listen to me!"

Nobody listens.

"Please, you don't understand..." I try again.

Again, nobody listens.

"GODDAMN IT, JUST LISTEN TO ME!!!" I finally shout, holding up the detonator, my finger on the button. "LISTEN TO ME OR SO HELP ME GOD I'LL BLOW US ALL TO HELL!!!"

Everyone finally shuts the hell up. They're frozen in place. Afraid to blink. Afraid to swallow. Dozens of wide, desperate eyes all falling on me.

"Good," I say. "Now, as I was trying to tell you before you all PANICKED like ALARMIST DOUCHEBAGS – although I suppose I *do* have a bomb strapped to my chest, so I guess your response was somewhat valid – but anyway, there is a perfectly reasonable explanation for this, and that perfectly reasonable explanation is..."

Suddenly, the entire bus jolts forward as a suped-up Range Rover rams us from behind. I lose my footing from the impact and nearly drop the detonator in the process.

"What the hell was that?" I scream, whipping around. The SUV is jackknifed into the side of the bus. Its hood crumpled and the radiator is coughing up steam.

"Dylan!" a familiar voice cries out from the tinted driver's side window. "Dylan, my sweet little cumrag! I've found you! I've finally found you!"

Will Smith climbs out through the Range Rover's sunroof and leaps onto the back of the bus. There's a small cut on his forehead leaking a single sanguine droplet of blood down the side of his face. He even bleeds like a movie star. Will Smith pounds at the bus's exterior and squishes his face against the glass.

SOMNAMBULANT

Attached to the ends of both arms are his *Cockhand* movie prosthetics – two wobbly, watermelon-sized dildos replacing his hands. They are both oiled up and ready to go.

"Dylan, it's me!" he screams, smashing a cock through the window. "It's Big Willy Style!"

"Holy shit! Cockhand is here!" one of the passengers exclaims. "We're gonna be alright! Cockhand has come to save us!"

Using the mushroom tips of his phallic appendages as crowbars, Will Smith pries the emergency door open and climbs on board.

"Baby," he says to me, tears welling up in his soft-crescent eyes. "Dylan, I've been searching everywhere for you! I should've known you'd been kidnapped and brainwashed by Al-Qaeda forces to carry out this dastardly terrorist act. In fact, that's the exact plot of my latest pornographic rom-com action thriller – *Zero Cock Thirty*."

"Will," I say to the actor, my tone softening as I take his penis-hands into mine. "I'm sorry, but I'm not gay. And I'm not in love with you. You're delusional and psychotic." I turn to everyone else on the bus. "And I'm not a terrorist. I'm just a regular guy. I'm just like all of you."

"If you're juss like us, then why are you covered with explosives?" the gangsta asks.

"Yeah," Will Smith nods in agreement. "If you're such a 'regular guy' then how come I'm so obsessively infatuated with you? And why are you all strapped up with bombs? Man, this whole situation reminds me of that *Fresh Prince of Bel-Air* episode where I had to get a tonsillectomy, and I was all scared and shit but at the last moment I find the strength to be a man and face my fears. Remember that?"

"Why does it remind you of that?" I ask.

He stares blankly at me. "Well...gee...I dunno. But that *was* a pretty good episode, right?"

"Everybody," I say, turning my attention back to the other passengers, "I didn't wake up this morning intending to suicide bomb the Lincoln Tunnel. I didn't mean to have sex with Will Smith and make him fall in love with me. I didn't want to cut off my poor mama's arms when I was 13. It's just...sometimes I *do* things. In my sleep. And I don't remember how or why I did them. It's confusing and scary. As scary for me as it is for you. Maybe even more so. You've got to believe me when I say that I'm not the bad guy here. *I'm* the victim too!"

"You? The suicide bomber? You think *you're* the victim?"

"Yes!" I shout, "Just like you. And you. And you. And even you too, Will Smith. I've suffered. I'm out of control. I've been crash-landing for so goddamned long now, it's all I really know. I've been victimized. Brutalized. Traumatized. Subjugated over and over again by the world around me. A world I have no control over. I'm just a peon. A nobody. An afterimage on a TV set. And you can sit there and judge me if you think that'll help rationalize all the decisions you've made yourself. You can sit there and think about how you've 'got it all together.' How you're above a monster like me. But answer me this – who is it that is piloting your life? Whose path are you following? You work hard, you stay in school, get a good job, marry, procreate, live in a nice sterile house in a nice sterile suburb, you vacation at Disney, barbeque in the summer, drink a glass of red wine because they say it's good for your heart, private school for the kids then a Jesuit college, you get old, retire, Boca Raton, cancer, die. Now I'm not saying this is the wrong way to live. All in all, it sounds rather...*comfortable*, right? But the whole time you're going through these motions, how many of you are asking yourselves *why*? Why am I doing these things? Do they make me happy? Do they reflect who I am inside? Do you do them because you *want* to or because you're *supposed* to? Is the best you can hope for a normal, complacent life? I ask you good people of NJ Transit, how is complacency any different than sleepwalking? I've been all over the world – a thousand different cities and I've lived through a thousand different compromising situations – and the one thing I've learned is that we're all somnambulists, in our own way. Some of us wake up terrorist and some of us wake up with a 20-year mortgage on a two-story colonial in Basking Ridge. But I assure you all, whether it takes just one night or 60 goddamn years, eventually this sleep will end. You need to ask yourselves, right here and now – before you judge me, before you indict me, before you write me off as just a rambling madman hellbent on your imminent and ultimate destruction – on that day you finally do wake up, when you look in the mirror, are you gonna like the person you see staring back at you?

"Nice speech, Dylan Spotter," a quroot-soured voice from the front of the bus suddenly interrupts. Everyone turns. Standing in the doorway is the triple-headed Osama Bin-Laden/Saddam Hussein/Kim Jong-il monstrosity. "You pathetic piece of subhuman dick meat. You think we would've entrusted *you* with our most sacred mission without a contingency plan? Bwah-ha-ha-ha-ha! You're even dumber than Kimmy here looks."

"Hey! I am Sexiest Man of Millennium for All of Time as voted by media outlets across the world!" Kim Jong-il retorts.

"You fool," says Bin-Laden, addressing me. "You've already *completed* your mission."

"What are you talking about?" I go.

"You see, Dylan," Saddam Hussein says. "We are three of the most renowned terrorists in the entire history of terrorism..."

"We #1 Terrorist A-OK!" says Kim.

"People expect this kind of behavior from us," Saddam says. "But you? You were our secret weapon. Our symbolic weapon. Don't you see, Dylan? This is the ultimate statement. The ultimate terror. All-American Dylan Spotter in his Levis blue jeans and Converse sneakers – how could he defect? How could he turn on his own country? How can someone who looks like *you* be capable of something so heinous? Well, if Dylan Spotter can be a terrorist – then anyone can be a terrorist. NO ONE is safe. Fear! Paranoia! Chaos! After today, you're whole shitty way of life will be cast into doubt. And in doubt you shall crumble. In doubt you will fall!"

"You've served your purpose well, Dylan," Bin Laden picks up where Saddam left off. "But you were always just a cog in the wheel. You had to get the bomb down here. And when the government and media review the footage of this day – when they piece it all together from traffic cams and security feeds, they'll see you, your happy stupid face as you carry the payload. As you wait at the Greyhound station. As you step onto the bus. Any one of us could've planted a bomb on this bus. But only a pale-faced white boy can make the statement we truly needed to make. *Ka-BOOM!* The whole world shall hear our song. And you, Dylan, are the catalyst of the New World Odor."

"Don't you mean New World *Order*?" Will Smith brazenly interrupts.

Kim Jong-il, in control of the one arm at his disposal, draws a large-bore semiautomatic pistol, aims it at the actor, and squeezes the trigger. Will Smith lets out a yelp as the bullet pierces his shoulder. "Arrrggh...that's my good shoulder, you douche! I need that for busting through doors in my films and shit. Man, this whole fucked-up day totally reminds me of that scene in *The Legend of Bagger Vance* where my character blows Matt Damon's character for like, six hours straight, except this ain't nothing like that and is not happening in my head only."

"Holy crap!" someone shrieks, "I can't believe you just shot Will Smith!"

"What-fuckin'-ever, bitch," replies Bin-Laden. "My point is that it's *time*, Dylan. Press the button. You must WAKE the American people UP!!! You must explode the tunnel! It is the only way! For we are the righteous, ordained by Br'Khuna Himself! The whole world must suffer! It is the only way!"

"It's not gonna happen, Osaddam Bin-Jongsein," I reply, giving the terrorist my best Bruce Willis stare. "I of all people can tell you – you can't just shake a sleepwalker awake. And you can't tell me what to do. It's morning. My eyes are open. I'm taking control. And I'm saying NO MORE BULLSHIT!!!"

"*Tsk tsk tsk*," clucks Bin-Laden. "Such a shame you couldn't have just accepted things the way they are. Welp, I suppose pain is the only call you're gonna answer to. Prepare to feel the wrath of our latest recruit, then..."

Kim's arm and Saddam's arm slowly reach down to open Osama's dishdasha. From within the thick, wiry black hairs comprising the Superterrorist's pubic mound, the head of a balding Chinese man emerges on the end of a long, veiny shaft – a greasy and throbbing giraffe's neck of an erection with the face of Communist dictator Mao Zedong at its tip. He smiles at me – a vicious, shark-toothed smile, rank piss and acidic pre-cum dripping from his mouth in the place of saliva.

"Mao Zedong?" I ask, in disbelief.

"It's Mao *thee Dong* now," the Chairman says. "And I'm about to commit genocide on your candy ass!"

The massive penis monster slowly snakes toward me, twisting deftly down the aisle like a herpetic ball of python. Osama, Kim, and Saddam are all laughing like the trio of comic book villains they are – *BWAHAHAHAHAHAHAHAHA!!!* –

SOMNAMBULANT

as Mao thee Dong gnashes his purple peehole and lunges at me like a rattlesnake about to strike. I turn to run, but the mass of terrified people are blocking my path. I spin back around and face the monster cock. Closing my eyes, I accept the fact that I'm about to be this mutant dicktator's lunch when, all of a sudden...

"...pass på verden, her over JEG komme!" I hear his Nordic voice crow, quickly followed by the unholy rumble of his gas-starved motor. I turn just in time to see a man racing toward us on a dirt bike. He pops a wheelie, flies over the top of an Italian sports car, and smashes through the back of the bus in a maelstrom of splintered glass and exhaust fumes. Screeching to halt mere inches from my toes, the psychotic stuntman pulls off his helmet.

It's Asbjorn!

"Holy fuckballs!" Osama Bin-Laden exclaims. "That was crazy! You drove that motorcycle right into the bus. I mean, obviously I think you're an infidel and you should die and all that kinda stuff, but I gotta give credit where credit is due, bro. That was awesome as hell – just like a movie!"

"True," Will Smith interjects. "Same thing happened in my action movie classic *The Pursuit of Happyness*." He stops to think for a second. "Or was it the sequel *The Pure Suit of a Penis*? Man, I really gotta lay off the peyote..."

"Asbjorn, what are you doing here?" I ask my long-lost friend.

"What are you meaning, Dylan? Are we friends or are we not? I have come to save the day and save these people from whatever the hell that thing is," he says, pointing to Mao thee Dong.

"You're too late, you Swedish meatball," growls Chairman Mao. "The four of us terrorists combined? We're too powerful! Nothing can stop us – everyone will suffer. EVERYONE!!!"

"I'm Norwegian, you pathetic malformed peckerfaced cockknob!" shouts Asbjorn, drawing a long-barreled magnum revolver from his trousers and pointing it right at the Superterrorist's eye.

"What the heck? C'mon, dude. Be cool," Saddam Hussein says.

"Can you hear it, Dylan," goes Asbjorn, turning to me. "Can you hear the alarm clock ringing?"

"But..." I begin.

"Just take the vest off," Asbjorn says, still holding the dictators at gunpoint. "Just lay it down. You do not need to carry a responsibility such as this. All the Will Smiths and terrorists, all the art thieves and tribal chiefs – none of this is the fault of your own. You are just one man doing his best to navigate a world out of his control. As are we all one men navigating our own worlds. Perhaps that is lesson to be learned in all of this. Perhaps sleepwalking is not so bad. In sleep you can dream. The American Dream, no? Take off the vestings you are wearing and let us just walk away."

"Fuck that! Fulfill your destiny as a vessel of the New World Odor, and live forever as a martyr!" Bin-Laden cuts in. "Your flesh is temporary, Dylan. Your actions, forever. Wake up the world..."

"I...I..." I stutter, slowly stepping backward, "I'm gonna..."

And then, before I can finish my sentence, I slip in a puddle of something white and gooey. And as I fall to the floor, I catch a glimpse of Will Smith standing behind me, pants around his ankles, a long strand of semen connecting his waning erection to the pool of spunk beneath me.

"Goddamn it, Will!" I cry out as my legs flail helplessly under my body. "Your sperm has doomed us all!"

"I'm sorry, Dylan," he weakly replies, his soft brown eyes containing all the sadness of the world.

I fall and connect with the ground.

The button on the detonator pushes in.

There comes a quiet beep.

And then the bomb explodes.

SOMNAMBULANT

<u>TOMORROW</u>

When I wake up, the vanilla tendrils of the honey-colored sun are pouring in through an open window, mixing with the breeze in the same way that chocolate chips mix with cookie dough – so sweet and perfect together, my eyelids open as if I were ice-creamed in consciousness. I melt awake.

The room I'm in seems familiar. Pastel-peach walls. Pink sheets. Stuffed white bears. The scent of floral perfume wafting all around me...

I quickly sit up and look around, but she's nowhere to be seen.

"Hello?" I call out. "Hello? Are you here?"

Then I hear her coming down the hall, the soles of her bare feet lightly slapping the wood floor, soft and rhythmic, like a distant drum. My adrenaline starts pumping; all the electricity in my body charging to the surface of my skin like an army pushing against a castle gate. The oxygen in the room evaporates and I can't breathe. I'm cryogenic. I'm in a vacuum. I'm on the moon until she appears there in the doorway to her bedroom, as radiant and beautiful as I've remembered her. As she was in my dreams. She's wearing just a button-down shirt with no pants or socks, her bare-skinned legs filling up the heavenly space between her hips and the floor. She pushes her hair behind her ear and smiles at me.

"Hey there, sleepyhead," she says.

"I can't believe it," I reply, my voice trembling. "I've found you. I've finally found you!"

"Well, that's just a matter of perspective," she says, "isn't it?" She sits beside me on the bed, giving me a kiss on the cheek. "I like to think we found each other."

"You have no idea what I've been through," I go, my eyes welling up with tears. "How much I had to endure, just to wake up here once more."

"Oh, I may have a *bit* of an idea," she says, pulling out a scrapbook filled with newspaper clippings. I quickly scan a few of the headlines:

103

Danger_Slater

ISLAND LEADER SAYS MESSIAH ORDAINED THEIR SOVEREIGNTY

WILL SMITH TO MARRY NORWEGIAN MAN IN SMALL CIVIL CEREMONY

COCKATOO SHIT: THE MIRACLE CURE?

Flipping to the last page in the book, she directs my attention to the most recent article:

MYSTERY HERO STOPS NYC TUNNEL TERROR PLOT

"But the bomb went off," I say, unbelieving.

"Actually, it didn't," she replies.

"But...I slipped and the detonator got pushed in. The bomb exploded right in my face. I'm pretty sure I died."

"You're not dead, silly," she says. "The bomb got so caked up with Will Smith's cum that none of the triggers worked. You must've gotten yourself into such a tumult that you fainted or something. From the looks of it, it's been a rough couple of weeks for you. You probably just needed some rest."

"So what happened then?" I ask.

She shrugs. "I don't know. The details in the article are a bit sketchy...suffice it to say that The Post quoted Will Smith as saying it was 'without a doubt the *weirdest* orgy I've ever been to.'"

"Oh Jesus," I say, burying my face in my hands for a moment before regaining my composure. I look at my left palm. My pinky-less palm. "So what about the terrorists then? Osama Bin-Laden and Kim Jong-il and the rest of 'em? Don't tell me they escaped..."

"Well..." she wavers, "I mean..."

"Goddamn it," I reply, slamming my fist against my thigh. "I was so close to stopping them. I could've made a real difference in the world."

She smiles at me. "Dylan, you *are* making a difference in the world."

104

SOMNAMBULANT

I smile back. "Hey, do you remember what you said to me last time I was here? About how we can never really touch anything? About how, molecularly at least, we're all doomed to forever be apart?

"Of course," she goes. "What about it?"

"You were wrong," I flatly say.

"I was?" she asks.

"Yeah, you were. You were wrong because here you are again, right in front of me. You were wrong because, if you keep grasping, keep fighting, keep pushing hard enough against the grain, then one day you're bound to connect with something. Even if it's only temporary. Even if it's for just a day. In the end, that's pretty much the best any of us can hope for."

She takes my hand in hers and gives it a tender squeeze.

"C'mon, Dylan. Wake up. I made us some breakfast."

I get out of bed and briefly catch the image of my reflection in the mirror. My chest is covered in scrapes and lacerations, as are my face and shoulders and back. In fact, my entire body is a roadmap of scars, crisscrossing my skin like little highways. Proof, I guess – of what I've done. Of what I've endured. Of what I *can* endure.

Proof that I existed.

And I continue to exist.

I throw on some pajama bottoms and follow her into the kitchen. Fresh pancakes and strawberries are already on the table. Syrup. Sausage. Bacon and eggs. My stomach rumbles. I can't recall the last time I actually sat down for breakfast.

She carries a pan over and drops a piece of French toast onto my plate. Hanging on the kitchen wall next to me is Edvard Munch's *The Scream*. The macaroni man looks still just as tortured as he's ever been. As he's destined to always be. But, I think, perhaps that's okay. Perhaps he's there to remind us that it's okay to scream. To keep screaming. To scream eternal. And maybe, just maybe, this morning he's woken up a little bit wiser, a little bit calmer, a little bit happier than he was yesterday.

One has to hope, right?

So I give him a wink and a nod. Keep keepin' on, brother.

We've all had those days.

"Bon appétit," she says, cheersing me with a mug of hot coffee. I cheers her back.

Today's gonna be a good one.

But who knows where we'll wake up tomorrow.

ME & ME & ME & ME & ME & ME & ME & ME

a novella by Danger_Slater

Hell is other people

—Jean-Paul Sarte

<u>CHAPTER ONE</u>

Okay, I'll admit it. It gets a little lonely from time to time.

Don't roll your eyes at me like that. I know, I know. I shouldn't be complaining. And I'm not. Not officially, at least. All things considered, I've got it pretty good up here in The Pod. Downstairs, things can get a bit...messy. There's war and pollution and poverty and crime. There's cancer and climate change and xenophobia and death. Anxiety and acne and ignorance and tsunamis and toxic waste and zealotry and obesity and rape and the hole in the ozone keeps getting bigger and bigger and the oil reserves are quickly running dry and the population is exploding faster than agricultural resources can be renewed and the plastic in the ocean is killing all the fish and assault weapons and papercuts and terrorism and slavery and hurricanes and earthquakes and burnt toast and apathy...

Downstairs is chock-full of all that kind of icky stuff. But I don't have to tell you. *You're* the one stuck on Earth. You know exactly what I'm talking about. It must be terrible, having to live in constant fear. Knowing that this is the world you helped create. On a monster planet, everyone's a Frankenstein. Well shit, man, what kind of birthright is that? There's a lot of guilt there. I know I wouldn't like it one bit.

Of course, up here in The Pod, those are not my worries. Up here in The Pod, it is serene.

Danger_Slater

So I look out the small porthole at the stars – the innumerable sparkling stars that spread out across the breadth of space like a geyser of unblinking eyes bubbling forth from the darkness. Millions of eyes. *Billions* of eyes. Billions and billions of eyes eternal – all watching me in much the same way that the billions and billions of eyes back home on Earth are watching me. I'm their last hope. I'm *your* last hope. Our planet is dying. I've been sent to find us a new one. I am the salvation for all mankind, floating alone across the endless void of space.

Down there they call me a hero. Up here I'm called nothing. In The Pod there's just me.

Only me.

CHAPTER TWO

On the agenda today: recalibrate the thermal regulator, disinfect the lavatory filters, reset the air revitalization rack.

"Mission! Mission! Come in, Mission!" I cry out.

"Go ahead, Almond," crackles Mission Control over the ship's intercom. It echoes down the ship's empty corridors and resonates off its titanium hull, echoes upon echoes, until the voice surrounds me on all sides as if it were a blanket of sound draped over my shoulders.

"I just cut my finger off on the damned table track!" I shout, as my finger goes floating past my head. Globules of hot crimson blood follow close behind it like the tail of a comet. With my good hand I switch on the ship's Vacuuclean system. Apertures running along each wall click open with a high-pitched whirr, sucking the plaintive, solemn drops of blood out of The Pod and ejecting them into space like tiny frozen rubies. My finger twirls lopsided like a cock-eyed moon, dancing its way toward one of the vacuum holes, but just as it's about to vanish forever into outer space, I snatch it out of the air and shove it into my pocket.

"How bad is it, Almond?" asks Mission Control.

"Just one finger. Left ring. I told you guys that this retractable table was a bad idea." I say, calming down a bit. "Not much blood loss, but it hurts like a motherfucker. Who built this stupid thing, anyway? The table track is always getting jammed up. It's a real pain in my ass!"

"I thought it was your finger that was amputated?"

"Ha ha, very funny..."

There's a brief pause. "So which one was amputated? Your finger or your ass?"

"My finger!" I go.

"Please don't raise your voice, Almond. We're only trying to get the facts straight." Mission Control flatly says. "And as far as the table goes, I'm sure you're aware that The Pod was not designed by *Good Housekeeping*. It was built to be as utilitarian and efficient as possible. The table slides in and out of the wall to save on space."

"Right, I understand that, but..."

"It didn't sound like you understood that when you were slandering the table only moments ago."

"My humble apologizes, Mission," I say.

There's another pause and I can hear the person on the other end of the loudspeaker tapping away at a keyboard.

"All right then," Mission eventually goes. "You are now authorized to use the refabricator. It's not a huge wound, so regeneration should only take a few minutes. In the future, do try to be more careful, Almond. You have a lot of people down here counting on you."

"I know that, Mission. I will not let you down."

The intercom clicks off, as does the Vacuuclean system. For a moment, the whole ship is eerily quiet. I gently clear my throat, temporarily reassured by the broken silence.

I make my way over to the refabricator, switch it on and shove my hand inside. It beeps and whirls as it uploads my DNA coding. Then comes the sting. Like needles or fire or a swarm of angry bees, my hand erupts into a volcano of concentrated pain. I grit my teeth and bear it with as much composure as I can possibly muster, but it hurts like hell. Two whole minutes of hell. Two whole minutes of hell I must endure, a pain far worse than severing my finger in the first place, until the refabricator finally emits an exonerative *ding*. I pull out my still-tingling hand, holding it up to my face as I wiggle my fingers. A full five nimble digits wave back at me, including my freshly regenerated ring finger. Good as new. Better than new, actually.

Newer. Newest!

ME & ME & ME & ME & ME & ME & ME & ME

I pat my pocket where my original finger sits.

I suppose it never hurts to have a spare.

CHAPTER THREE

It's all been leading to this. This mission. My entire life has been in preparation of this exact moment.

I am here to save the world.

All right, perhaps I'm exaggerating a bit here. My involvement in Project Eden isn't nearly as altruistic as it is...circumstantial. But circumstance doesn't preclude me from greatness, does it? I mean, that's the part of the Bible that no one ever talks about. Jesus never chose to be a Jesus, after all. He was just born one.

My mother and father were handpicked by an official conglomernmental genealogical research team out of roughly two million other highly qualified pairs. They were chosen for their mental and physical prowess, as well as their general intellectual aptitude and all-around problem-solving skills. Genetically, they were the best the human race had to offer. And I was to be their product. Their child. And not just their child, but *the* child of all humanity. The end result of a trillion years of evolution. Mankind's perfect son. The paradigm.

They conceived me in a conglomernment-sanctioned procreation bunker on June 8th, 2143, and I was born into the world on March 18th of the following year.

I never met my parents. Not personally, at least. I've seen their pictures. Read the magazine articles, interviews. Watched their TV spots. They were famous in their own right, and deservedly so. After all, it was their seed from which I was sprung. Without them, there'd be no me. But let's not kid ourselves – they weren't nearly as famous as *I* am now. No one downstairs is. I'm instantly recognizable to every man, woman and child the whole world over. They write comic books about me. Sell T-shirts adorned with my felicific face. I'm on Coke cans and Wheaties boxes and my name is synonymous with the word 'hero.'

But my parents? Not so much. Sure, they get an interview here or a photo spread there, but it's nothing like the commendation that I regularly receive. Is that fair? I mean, they played a big part in all of this, don'tcha think? I sometimes feel like they deserve a piece of Eden, too. As do their parents. And their parents before them. Their parents' parents. And their parents' parents' parents. And so on and so on, all the way back, through every single demure and depraved sexual act in my entire personal lineage, until we reach that very first man who one day decided to crawl out of that primordial muck and declare himself human. The muck man brave enough to stand up and claim the Earth as his home. And look at us now, stepping out even farther than that! Conquering the stars. Conquering the universe. All because of a little sex a million years ago...

Yessiree, a whole lot of fucking and sucking went on in the past, but they hardly ever mention that in the Bible either.

CHAPTER FOUR

Deep under the surface of the Earth, in the Al-Hajarah desert in what was formerly known as southern Iraq, there sat an ancient cave.

This cave was tucked away, far from human eyes, buried beneath ten thousand millennia's worth of sediment and rock, until about 35 years ago when it was discovered by a squadron of conglomernmental oil extraction specialists during a standard military fracking offensive. That day, they say the ground opened up like the mouth of God and swallowed half the platoon in one gulp. I wasn't quite born yet, so I can't speak to the facts; suffice it to say that whatever happened changed human history forever.

In this cave they found an extraordinarily long and complicated mathematical equation carved into the limestone walls. Once practically applied, this particular sequence of numbers is what led to nearly all mankind's technological advances of the past three decades. Without this equation, intergalactic space travel, the refabricator, the Qdoor, even The Pod itself, not to mention the combined sum of these things – mankind's only chance at survival and redemption – without these numbers, in this exact order, NONE of it would've ever come to pass.

We, the human race, are now capable of reaching unfathomably far distances across unimaginably vast space in unquestionably short periods of time. Light-years and parsecs and mega-parsecs alike have become just signposts on another Highway Eternal. Mile markers en route to destinations previously thought beyond our scientific capabilities, beyond our terrestrial grasp.

Of course, these numbers haven't answered any of the BIG questions about life, the meaning of it, or any of that kind of crap. Numbers never posit 'why.' They only ever ask 'why not.' I suppose the most pressing mystery would be who came up with this equation in the first place. Conspiracy theorists point to the usual suspects, of course: ancient astronauts, the Egyptians, Bigfoot, pranksters. A lone, unidentified, malformed humanoid skeleton also found in the cave has only served to fuel this kind of wild speculation. Genetic tests on the bones have concluded them to be of human origin, so that pretty much laid the Bigfoot theory to bed. Unless Bigfoot really *is* human, but that's a whole other ethical discussion that I'm afraid we don't have time for right now.

ME & ME & ME & ME & ME & ME & ME & ME

The real question, I suppose, is could ancient man have been that insightful? That forthwith? Did they know things back then that we're only just rediscovering today? How could that be possible? *Why* would it be possible?

In the end, I suppose it doesn't much matter who wrote it or why they wrote it or even where such a grand notion originated to begin with. All that matters is that it was there for us to find, and that we finally found it.

And that because of it, I will save us all.

CHAPTER FIVE

On the agenda today: test the pH balance in the water separator and make any necessary adjustments, assess the integrity of the midbay pressurized internal shutter system, participate in a televised interview with Chip Branson, Channel 487,352's most popular news anchor.

Chip Branson's face fills the screen in front of me, all silk ties and obtuse angles, like a billboard come to life. A plastic smile spreads across his plastic cheeks until all that's left on his plastic face are the hoofprints of thousand happy, plastic days – that glazed sort-of halcyon swagger that only fits comfortably on a person of Chip Branson's repute. Nary a blemish. Not a hair out of place. Truly, he is the model of physical perfection. Something to aspire to. Someone to laud.

His face fills the screen in front of me just as I assume my face fills in the screen in front of him just as I assume both our faces are filling television screens across the whole wide world. A billion copies of myself, all identical in every way. They move in unison, say the same things that I say. I wonder how many versions of me there are out there?

It's really kind of weird when you think about it.

It's even weirder to think about all those people watching me on TV right now. They can all see me, but I can't see them. To me, they're only as real as an idea, a collective *them*, a vague notion, existing nowhere besides a place inside my head. Existing only to vindicate what I've been sent out here to do. In The Pod I am one. My own country. My own planet. In The Pod I am Saturn and they are my rings. I'm a monolith, a bridge, a peak atop the prairie lands. In The Pod I am the undisputed heavyweight champion. In The Pod I am king!

"Welcome back, folks. If you're just tuning in, we're being joined via satellite by astronaut Abner Almond, whom I'm *sure* you all know from the infamous Project Eden. Good evening, Abner."

"Thanks for having me, Mr. Branson," I say.

"Mr. Branson was my father," says the anchorman with a smile. "Please, call me Mr. Chip Branson."

"Um...okay..."

"Now, Abner, for any viewers out there who might be completely sheltered-fucking-morons, why don't you briefly explain what Project Eden is to us?"

"I...don't think it's really fair to call people morons..."

"Well they are."

"But..."

"*Shhh!*"

"All right, then."

"So as you were saying, Abner..."

"Right," I begin, clearing my throat. "I suppose it should come as no surprise to anyone when I say that planet Earth is being stretched to its capacity. Natural resources are being rapidly depleted while the population keeps exponentially increasing. There's simply not enough habitable land for everyone. Project Eden is an inter-conglomernmental space travel endeavor funded by various multinational corporations for the propagation and benefit of all mankind."

"So what part do you play in all this?" asks Chip. "Are you there to battle any space squids that threaten the mission?"

"Haha, well, nothing quite so dramatic, I'm afraid...as many of you know, I have been trained, literally since birth, to man and maintain The Pod – that's the name of my ship here – the sole purpose of which is to transport the Qdoor to XJ4-111Z-1 as smoothly and safely as possible. The Pod itself is equipped with a state-of-the-art navigation unit, monitored by Mission Control down there on Earth, and is guided through the cosmos using an advanced hyper-intuitive autopilot system. I'm really here just to make sure nothing goes wrong on this side of the galaxy. To be honest, I'm more of a glorified janitor than an astronaut."

"The Qdoor? What's that?"

"That, Mr. Branson..."

Chip abruptly clears his throat.

"...Mr. *Chip* Branson, the Qdoor – short for *quantum doorway* – is basically the whole reason why this mission exists. To put it simply, it's a teleportation device. Once we make landfall on XJ4-111Z-1, I'm to run a few environmental tests, but if our current data is correct, the air should be breathable and the flora and fauna should be quite similar to what we had on Earth around the mid-Cenozoic period. I will flip the switch and open the passage from this planet to that one. After that, travel between the two should be as easy as stepping from one room into another. Then colonization of XJ4-111Z-1 can begin."

"XJ4-111Z-1? That's a mouthful, huh? Imagine having to say that all the time?"

"Well, I *do* have say it all the time."

"It's too long and stupid. I'm just gonna call it Earth 2. You cool with that?"

"I mean, I don't have the authority to say yes or no, but Earth 2 is a bit of a misnomer..."

"So, Earth 2 then?"

"Well..."

"Good. I'm glad we're in agreement."

"But..."

"So, where were we? Oh right! Abbey – you don't mind if I call you Abbey, do you Abbeybaby? – exactly how looooooong is this mission from Earth 1 to Earth 2 supposed to take anyway, Abbeybabycakes?"

"The total trip was to take approximately two years from the time of my departure to the moment of touchdown. Of course, we launched nearly two years ago already, so, according to my watch, in exactly 11 days, 4 hours, 23 minutes, and 54 seconds, I should be stepping off The Pod and onto XJ4-111...er, I mean, Earth 2."

"And what do you say, SweetlittleAbbeybabycakes, to the critics of Project Eden who say that this sort of over-ambitious, idealistic and *expensive* undertaking is a waste of conglomernmental funds – funds that could be spent on something like...oh, I don't know...building a giant statue or bolstering national defense or something?"

"In a way, Chip, this *is* national defense. All scientific advancement is national defense. Not in the jingoistic, us-versus-them kind of way, but more like a defense against the follies we've committed against *ourselves* as a species. Earth is in a period of turmoil, as anyone out there listening to this can attest. The planet will die, as all planets do. We're carving a path, bushwhacking our way across a new frontier, taking the necessary steps to secure a future for the human race in this Universe. If you think about it, this is really less of a defense and more of an offense. We're not going to strip our soil and pollute our air and poison our water and irradiate our bodies without a back-up plan in place, after all."

"But surely, Mr. Almond..."

"What do you do, Mr. Chip Branson, when your ship is sinking? You get on another ship, that's what you do. In this endless ocean of stars, in this infinite Universe, as long as you can keep your head above water, there is always still hope."

CHAPTER SIX

"Mission. Mission, are you there?"

"Yes, Almond?" comes Mission Control's voice over the loudspeaker, cutting through the radio static. It's kinda crazy to think how far the words we speak have to travel just to be heard. The voice of Mission Control is digitized, then atomized, then blasted across the vast open nothingness between me and my home planet, just so my lonely little ship can intercept its message, reassemble it piece by piece, and turn all those tiny little molecules back into a human voice saying human words. Like the bricks comprising the great pyramids of Egypt, this conversation is our record, our legacy, our offering to the gods, our proof, our moment, our last will and testament, and our tomb.

"Mission," I ask, "what would you do if I died?"

"Excuse me?" Mission replies.

"If something went wrong. Say, the airlock blew and I was sucked out into space, or a rogue meteor struck The Pod or something. Or let's say my heart suddenly decided to crap out and I unexpectedly expired. What would you do?"

"You're heart is not going to 'crap out,' Almond. You were cultivated to be the very model of perfect health."

"I know my heart won't just stop," I go. "I'm just saying, *what if* it happened?"

"Well..." says Mission, "I suspect there would be a brief moment of shock, which would soon segue into disappointment, which would then be followed by a short period of mourning. There would probably be a service – televised, of course. People would want closure like that. Maybe they'd create a memorial for you – a statue or a plaque on a park bench or something. But probably not. Truthfully, if you died, that means you would've *failed* your mission, and they don't usually give plaques on park benches to failures. Most likely you'll end up a footnote in the encyclopedia, a sentence or two at the bottom of the page written for the person who actually delivers the Qdoor to

XJ4-111Z-1. There are other astronauts on standby, after all. I'm sure each and every one of them would jump at the chance to be commemorated as a hero."

"Yeah, I understand that's what the congolmernment would do...I understand I'm replaceable from a technical standpoint, but what about you, Mission Control? Personally. I mean, would you feel sad?"

There is a pause.

"Appropriately sad, I suppose."

"Appropriately sad?"

"Time keeps moving forward, Almond," Mission Control says. "We are all just tomorrow's dust, waiting to happen. And I don't weep for dust. I wipe it away and move on."

I sigh deeply.

"Do you love me, Mission?" I meekly, almost desperately, ask.

There is another pause, longer than the last one, before Mission Control finally replies, "No."

CHAPTER SEVEN

On the agenda today: complete assembly on the Node-3 baseplate ballast, inspect the CBM panel for anomalies...

...pants around my ankles, I climb perilously onto the same retractable table that severed my finger only days before. "Ugh, uhnn, urmmm," I softly moan as I gently hump the ever-loving shit out of The Pod's Vacuuclean system.

"*Wwwwhhhirrrrr*" the Vacuuclean replies as it blows me.

Now look, before you label me as some sort of sex pervert, I just want you to realize that I'm not fucking this vacuum cleaner out of any sort of physical or psychological attraction to it. That'd be weird. I fuck the Vacuuclean because my very nature dictates that I do so. Don't shake your head. You know what I'm talking about. I'm just a human. And humans are filthy, filthy creatures. We shit and puke and sweat and piss. We pull those long crusty boogers out of our noses when we assume that no one is looking. And we cum. We *have to* cum. I *know* you know what I mean. It's hardwired. Built in. A biological imperative, nearly just as urgent as eating. Or breathing. It's almost as necessary as my heartbeat itself.

I may not have had the same experiences as you. I may not have been to all the same places you've been to or seen all the same things you've seen, but I'm still a man, am I not? Yes, I am a man and I don't think it's very fair for you to sit there all comfy on the surface of the Earth and judge me for my lifestyle choices. You probably have a wife or a husband or some sort of significant other that helps you fulfill this most base of desires. Your options for sexual partners aren't exactly limited to the hull of a spaceship. And even then – even when you have an entire planet's worth of other filthy humans to aide you in relieving this most lascivious of longings – I'm sure a fair number of you have *still* tried to bang some random hole in some random appliance. And I understand. I truly do. I'm sure that as long as holes in things have existed, people out there have been trying to have sex with them.

And as for this hole in particular? Let me tell you – to feel a vacuum unrelentingly suck you off, applying the most even of pressures to all the right places? To feel the coolness of outer space on the tip of your penis? To literally *fuck* the *void*? Sure, it's caused me some mild frostbite and bit of chafing here and there, but it's still the closest thing to a woman I've ever had.

"Do you love me? Do you love me, Vacuuclean system?"

"*Wwwwhhhirrrrrr.*"

"You too, Vacuuclean. I love you too..."

It's Tuesday afternoon and I'm somewhere alone in the middle of the Universe, perched on top of a retractable table, fucking this vacuum cleaner senseless when all of a sudden communications cut out.

A high-pitched shriek escapes from the intercom like an aural locomotive, crashing straight into my unprotected ear canals. I tumble off the table and onto the floor, trying unsuccessfully to cover my ears and pull up my trousers at the same time. In a fit of desperation, I scramble over to The Pod's central control panel.

"Mission!" I scream, "Mission Control, what is that ungodly sound?"

The shrieking seems to grow even louder in response. I can feel my nose start to bleed as the pressure mounts inside my head. My eyes begin to bulge and my entire body shakes.

"Grraaahhh!!!" I cry as the blood pours out of my eyes, mouth and ears. I curl up on the hard metal floor, fetal and helpless. And just when I think I can't stand it anymore, just when I think my skull will surely explode, wallpapering The Pod's interior with my scrambled brains, the shrieking suddenly stops just as abruptly as it began.

"Mission, what the hell was that?" I gasp into the microphone, clawing my way back up to the switchboard. "What was that sound?"

There's no response.

"Mission? Mission? Come in, Mission! Come in!"

Still nothing. Not even the static hiss of dead air. I move some wires around and toggle a few switches.

123

"Mission, are you receiving me? I think something happened to the speaker system. Mission, are communications out? Mission? Mission?"

"..."

"Is there anybody out there?"

Silence.

CHAPTER EIGHT

On the agenda today: run a diagnostic scan on the entire ship to determine the cause of last week's communications failure, identify and rectify the problem, balance the south chamber depressurization probe.

There are procedures in place for this. Any number of computer malfunctions are indeed possible, even likely, and my training for this mission had prepared me for as much. I run through all the various scenarios, one by one, hoping that a solution will present itself.

So could a rogue chunk of space debris, maybe a miniature meteor or a fractal of an asteroid, have struck the radio hub on The Pod's exterior, damaging, disrupting, or otherwise cutting off all communications with Earth? It's certainly possible, but the chances of a meteor approaching without setting off any of the ship's impact-detection sensors, then striking the tiny piece of equipment responsible for connecting me to Mission Control (without damaging the vessel's structural integrity, mind you), only to disappear back into the blackness of space without so much as a peep? Very, very low.

Maybe it's some form of cosmic interference. An emission of concentrated electromagnetic energy emanating from a distant quasar. That very easily could interfere with The Pod's radio broadcast. Of course, any EMP large enough to affect the ship's communication system would've surely affected all of the other electronic systems as well, such as my lights and oxygen. Also, any EMP large enough to devastate The Pod on such a scale surely would've also been large enough to fry my entire endocrine system and cook the rest of me alive as well.

More than likely, it was a system failure back on Earth. As technologically advanced we as a society like to think we've come, no amount of planning can eliminate all possibility of user error.

Now, as to what may have caused a systems failure on Earth, I can only speculate. But I'm sure they'll have things back up and running in no time.

Right?

CHAPTER NINE

On the agenda today: continue efforts to determine cause of communications failure six months ago, take steps necessary to rectify the problem, spend some 'quality' time with Vacuuclean.

I throw a fishstick and a spot of OJ into the refabricator and hit the 'copy' button. The machine honks and trills, whistles and blares as the cooling fan sucks in air. I hear the tiny *boom boom boom* of millions and millions of miniscule molecules being disassembled and built back up again like a subatomic London Bridge connecting the River Thames to my supper.

Ding.

Taking out the freshly replicated fishsticks and orange juice, I sit down at my retractable table to eat.

I should've made landfall on XJ4-111Z-1 about five months ago. The autopilot system should've carried me to my destination whether communications were out or not. That must mean that guidance and navigation are out too, both of which are directed by Mission Control back on Earth. I wonder what could've happened to cause such a grievous error that it's taking this long to get everything back online. Was it a sunspot? A fire? Budget constraints down at HQ?

Or worse...

No. No, no, no, let's not head down that road. We must stay positive. Think happy thoughts. While this is certainly not the outcome I would've desired, it surely was a possibility.

Six weeks was the longest I ever spent in the isolation chamber back on Earth. That was how I spent my seventh birthday. No cake. No party. No presents or hugs. Just darkness and silence and me and me and me and me and me and me and me and me.

Listen, if you're thinking myopically here, you're probably going to equate the conglomernment sticking a seven-year-old boy in solitary confinement for 'research' purposes with pure and simple torture. And as a general rule, you'd probably be right. After all, if it wasn't the conglomernment doing it and it was, say, the quiet guy who lives down the hall in 6F, it *would* be considered torture. I survived it. And, objectively speaking, I can see the value in what they did. I understand why it had to happen. But if we're being honest with each other, and I think I have been so far, it *did* kind of feel a little like torture while I was going through it. Look, I'm not questioning my orders here. I know it was for the greater good. I know the ends are going to justify the means and once this computer malfunction gets fixed and Project Eden is complete, it will be *me* who saves the world!

Just like a superhero or something. Almond Man!

But what they *don't* tell you, what they *don't* report in the magazines and on TV is this: Something happens to you when you spend all that time alone. Something both strange and profound. You begin to change – but not in any drastic or overt way. You change just a little. Subtly. Isolation sort of peels off a layer of the stuff that connects you to the rest of humanity, while at the same time adding a new layer on top of what makes you *you*. Not that prolonged isolation is a foolproof formula for making a person more introspective or spiritual or thoughtful or anything like that. It just...it forces you to retreat into yourself for company. It makes you confront your own head.

I guess the only problem there is that your head isn't necessarily always someone you'd care to meet.

CHAPTER TEN

On the agenda today: contemplate the futility of everything, continue the slow march towards death, ennui, rue.

Nine whole years since I last had contact with the outside world.

One hundred and eight months I've been alone.

That's 3,287 days of loneliness.

78,888 hours of isolation.

4,733,280 minutes of seclusion.

283,996,800 seconds of unexplained solitude I've been forced to endure. Nearly an entire decade's worth of silence enveloping me ever since communications went dark. Since I last heard another human voice. Mission Control. Chip Branson. Anyone. Even my own voice sounds strange on the rare instances I use it. It echoes in my head. Distant vibrations like ocean waves upon foreign shores I'll never dip my toes into again. The echo of my voice is alien. A stranger. An invader. No longer a part of me, but something else.

I tried to use the Qdoor. About seven years ago. I thought, maybe I could escape The Pod or warp back to Earth or...I don't know *what* I thought. But it doesn't even matter now, does it? It didn't work. I followed the procedural manual explicitly. I flipped all the right switches and twisted all the right levers. I knew I shouldn't have been messing with it. Not until I reached XJ4-111Z-1. That was my mission. That's why I was born. I knew that if I got the Qdoor to work and I was somehow able to transport myself back to Earth I would most likely be tried for treason. But I didn't care. It would be worth the sacrifice just to hear another human voice sentence me to death.

The machine powered on just as it had in the simulations. Its central portal flashed asunder with blinding light, like a dragon opening its eye for the very first time. Fiery, yet soft. Piercing, yet tepid. Violent, yet beckoning. My ticket home. I took a deep breath and stepped inside, into the wormhole. I stepped through the Qdoor and came right out the other side. Still in The Pod.

ME & ME & ME & ME & ME & ME & ME & ME

It didn't work.

It didn't goddamn work.

Nothing on this piece of shit ship seems to work.

CHAPTER ELEVEN

I'm not married.

I don't have any kids.

I never made any friends.

I don't even own a cat.

Before I would've called those kind of tethers frivolous. Distractions. Anchors holding me back to my dying world. But now I've come to realize that nobody mourns me. By this point, if Mission Control still exists, they've undoubtedly assumed I'm long dead. A frozen corpse floating across galaxies. A ghost. A shadow. An afterthought trapped forever in the mental tomb of their memories. A billion miles away from home. Their home. My...

...my home?

Is it? Or is *this* my home now? The Pod. Is *this* where I belong, where I've always belonged? Was my former planet ever mine to begin with?

My upbringing didn't exactly lend itself to forming lasting or sustainable relationships. I spent almost all of my childhood training with conglomernmental scientists. They weren't mean or anything like that, but they weren't particularly warm either. At best they were stoic; robots performing the duties they'd been brought in to perform. So that's what I learned. That's what I did, too. I learned to perform my duties without flummery or fanfare. I learned to value the mission above even myself. Above my own thoughts and feelings. And I never thought I'd need them. After all, my childhood until now, however unconventional, seems substantially less complicated than those who were forced to suffer a more "normal" existence. From what I've read in books and seen on TV, relationships can be tricky. They seem complicated.

I mean, there's all these people around, and not only do your feelings and reactions vary from person to person, but they're also constantly in flux. Forever changing and evolving, filling up corners of your personality like spilt paint. Coloring you. Tainting you. These relationships can sometimes become conflicted. They can be hateful. Full of fire. Sadness. Grief. Or, adversely, these relationships can be pleasant. Congenial. Friendly. Jocular. I even hear that sometimes, when you're in a relationship, you can feel so full of love that it's actually overwhelming. Your heart beats differently and your brain gets cloudy like you're on drugs. Love so strong it flows like a river, out of you in all directions, so much so that it can literally *change* how you perceive the world. And do you know what the trickiest part is? Most relationships are usually a combination of all these things. And all of these different relationships you share with all of these different people, they surround you like a blanket. A cocoon. A spider's web of emotion, forever connecting people to each other. Fragile, yet beautiful. And they're all trapped.

Or so they say.

I wouldn't know anything about that, and I suppose now I never will. I guess it's kind of funny; the man chosen to save mankind had so little in common with the rest of it.

No, wait. 'Funny' is the wrong word.

It's more like...sad.

Thing is, when you really take it all into consideration – when you take a step back, when you're on the other side of the universe, when you're somehow able to find the courage to let go of your ego and embrace the oneness that is you alone – you'll finally be able to see what I see. Reality in all its intransigent truth:

You are small and life is short and on a timeline of cosmic proportions, you are probably already dead.

Yes, I'm sorry my friend, but you are dead. You've been dead for quite some time. Now, I don't mention this because I get off on fucking up your day. And I don't want burst your bubble with this dark fact, but it's important for you to know. For you to realize. For you to understand where I'm coming from.

Life is short. Life is immeasurably, infinitesimally, uncompromisingly short. There have been innumerable moments that have passed before you were born and there will be an infinite number of moments that will pass long after you're dead. And even now, when you've somehow managed to rage against the Cimmerian shade and claw your way out of the chasm of eternal nothingness that makes up the majority of your time in the Universe – your life is so short you've barely managed to exist at all. But don't despair just yet, my fellow peons! Even in the face of all that, there is still one very precious thing you do get to claim. One thing that the Universe, however bleak, cannot take away. One very beautiful and fragile thing that will be yours to keep until you breathe your very last breath:

The present. Right now. It's yours. And mine. We get to borrow it for a bit. It's our only reward, our only escape from the abyss that exists on either side of the grave. Yes, against all odds, we've conquered the night! ME AND YOU AND EVERYONE ELSE WHO LIVES AND BREATHES! WE'RE ALIVE! WE'RE ALIVE! DO YOU UNDERSTAND WHAT THAT MEANS? This is our only chance to experience the Universe as conscious beings! It will end someday soon. Why would we waste a minute of that time not examining and contemplating the meaning of it all? Why would we choose not to fully experience all the dirty pleasures life has to offer? Why would we let the conglomernment raise us in a hyperbaric chamber and then blast us into space without so much as putting up a fight?

You're free. We're free.

WE ARE BOTH FUCKING FREE!

Aren't we?

I look to my left, then to my right. The poly-titanium walls of The Pod encircle me. Entomb me. What am I talking about? I am not free. I am trapped here. But only physically, right? Only my body. My flesh. They can't stop my mind. Not anymore. The conglomernment may have subjugated my body, but they've never controlled my thoughts!

So look, I've gone off on a bit of a diatribe here, I know. But listen, I need your opinion. You're impartial, yes? You wouldn't lie to me, would you? No? Good. Let me ask you a question then:

Have I – do you think my life has been a waste? I mean, I understand that I was supposed to play a very important role for all of them downstairs, and every moment of my life was dedicated to that one very particular goal, but from the look of things it's just not gonna happen anymore. And chances are I'm never going to see Earth again. So tell me – has it all been in vain? Was my life a waste of time? They sent me out here to save humanity, but my doing so – my acquiescence to the conglomernment, my allowing them to force that responsibility upon me – I had to give up something very fundamental within myself. I had to give up a piece of my own humanity. Don't you see? The people I was supposed to be saving? I'm not even one of them. I never was. I never got a chance to live. To *truly* live. Not like the rest of them. I never got the chance to be a real person. I've never even had sex, for god's sake! Not with another human, at least. Can you imagine that? A virgin astronaut, lost in space. What kind of people would send a 30-year-old virgin on a dangerous intergalactic mission without even letting him fuck someone first? And now look at me. I'm going to die a virgin astronaut out here. Alone. Yes, I am forever doomed to be alone. Forever alone, floating past distant suns and distant moons forever. I am distant and floating alone forever and ever. Do you understand what I'm saying to you? Can't you see how unfathomably depressing all of this is? Can you imagine it, in your mind's eye? Can you hear my voice? Make out the tone and inflection? Can you hear me at all? Huh? Can ya? Why are you just sitting there like a lump of shit while I spill my guts out like a goddamned lunatic? Why won't you answer me? What is wrong with you? WHY ARE YOU DOING THIS TO ME? EXPLAIN YOURSELF! WHY? WHY?!?!?!?!!?!?

My severed finger just sits there, strapped into the seat across from me. Inert. Decaying. Despite being stored in stasis all these years, the flesh around the bone has turned black and sinewy, crusted over like drying tar. Gray, dusty skin draped over gray, decomposing muscle. A cracked, inch-long nail extends from the tip of my disembodied digit like a crooked tombstone half-buried in the mud. The smell of death surrounds it like a winter's coat.

Am I...have I been...how long have I been talking to this finger? Jesus, what the hell is happening to me? Has it been minutes? Days? Years? I'm so confused. It's all jumbled together. What have I said? What were we talking about? Look, I'm sorry. Whatever happens, I'd just like you to know that I'm sorry. You know I never meant to cut you off. It was an accident! That stupid sliding table, I just thought it was a simple design flaw. This whole fucking ship is a design flaw. I never wanted to part from you. Or replace you. You're my friend, Finger. My only friend. The only friend I've ever had. If only I knew you felt the same way about me, maybe all this time wouldn't feel so worthless. If only I knew what you were thinking...

...I slowly turn to the refabricator.

Hmmmm. I wonder what would happen?

In the most rudimentary sense of the term, I suppose I could be considered a 'scientist,' too...isn't it my obligation to experiment then? To question? To learn? To figure this out? And shit, Finger, look at me: what do I have to lose?

I walk over to the machine and flip the switch.

CHAPTER TWELVE

The refabricator kicks on with a mechanical *clunk*. Like a leaf blower it sounds, full of compressed air and rusty gears and teeny tiny metal parts all twisting together under its plasticine shell. Twisting like ballroom dancers. Twisting like the very Universe itself – an oiled machine of the most magnificent design, running in complete and perfect harmony. That is, except for one very miniscule and superfluous component muddling up the engine like a grain of sand.

Me.

I stick my severed finger into the refabricator and hit the 'repair' button. The lights in The Pod blink, then go out.

The machine screams, high-pitched and painful, much like that last, dying whelp the comm-system burped up from Mission Control all those years ago. The whole ship starts to shake. The lights reboot, but they're running dim as the refabricator diverts energy from other parts of The Pod. Even my oxygen starts to feel a little thin as the air revitalization rack switches over to low-power mode.

The refabricator is now coughing up hot, billowy plumes of steam, thick and slimy. It hangs in front of me like a window shade. A wall of obfuscation. For a moment I worry that I might've overloaded the system. What if it breaks and I can no longer refabricate food? What if it explodes and blows out the wall, sucking everything, including me, out into space? What if it uses up all the rest of the ship's power and I end up suffocating here in The Pod – the littlest Ahab dragged into the deep here in the belly of the last great white whale? What the fuck was I thinking, anyway? That this machine could take my finger and make a whole new me? How stupid is that? How stupid am I? The human body is *way* too complex to replicate in full. What has this decade of isolation done to me? If I didn't know any better, I'd say I was starting to lose my shit!

And then the refabricator suddenly shuts off, all the apparatuses and instruments within slowly winding down. The air revitalization system returns to full power. The Vacuuclean switches back on and begins sucking the smoke out of the room. Gently the fog is pulled away, as if it were mere curtains and the play was about to start.

Danger_Slater

And that's when I see him, curiously looking around as he takes in his surroundings. My Finger. My giant human finger, rising up six feet tall. Just as tall as me. Still half-rotten, but with a new sheen of pink, a new layer of vitality on top of all the gray bits from before. He turns towards me and there, on the fingertip, is a face. A face identical to my own. He blinks his eyes. Nubby, malformed arms protrude from his sides, just below the first knuckle joint, and at the ends of those arms there are hands, and at the ends of those hands there are still more fingers. A finger with fingers. He looks down, wiggles and bends his own opposable digits for the very first time. A tiny smile creeps across his fetid, fingerprinted cheeks.

"Whoa," Finger says. "This is weird as hell!"

I have ducked behind the retractable sliding table, cowering, as it were, at the sight of this...this...thing. Finger sees me and slimes his way across the floor, leaving a trail of pink chunky gunk behind him. Not quite blood exactly, but some other kind of bodily goo. It smells awful, like vomit and shit and rotten meat and sweat. It is then that I sneak a peek over the retractable tabletop. Finger stares down at me quizzically.

"What in the hell are ya hiding for, Abner?" Finger says.

"What – what are you?" is all I can manage to sputter.

"Is this some sort of trick question?" Finger goes. "What *am* I? How vague can you possibly be? Do you mean that physically, figuratively, or existentially? Because those last two options are gonna take quite some time to figure out. After all, what are any of us, eh?" he says with a raised eyebrow. "As for the former, it should be pretty obvious at this point. Just what in the hell do I look like, Abner? I'm you!"

136

CHAPTER THIRTEEN

On the agenda today: WHAT THE FUCK IS GOING ON?

"You're not me," I say to Finger.

"Well, I'm not 100% you, but that much should be obvious. I mean, *look* at me for fuck's sake! I'm a giant half-rotten sentient human finger. You're all...normal and shit."

I slowly stand up from behind the table, keeping a comfortable distance between us.

"So what exactly are you then?"

"If you want to get all technical about it, then I guess I'm a clone. But not like a carbon copy clone you'd see in the movies. I'm more like a clone of just your finger."

"But...how?"

"Look, dude, I don't know any more than you do. And since we're both kinda made of the same shit, our minds are bound to work in a similar fashion. And since you're standing here dumbfounded, well then I'm dumbfounded too. Think of it this way: do you know how you got to be you in the first place? Do you know all the particular circumstances throughout history that allowed you to be Abner Almond and not someone else? Or all the circumstances that allowed you to be the exact Abner Almond you are right now? With the same thoughts you're thinking and the same feelings you're feeling? Of course not. One day you just *are*. Fortuitously, yes, as evident by this conversation. But the means are still a mystery."

After a pause in which I'm unable to articulate a coherent reply, Finger continues:

"Hey buddy, I don't know what you were expecting when you threw me into that thing, but if this wasn't the desired outcome, I do apologize."

"No," I manage to blurt out. "No, don't apologize. Really. I don't know *what* I was expecting when I stuck you in the refabricator. I've just been up here all alone for so long now that my thoughts have been getting a tad bit...muddy of late."

"Hey, don't beat yourself up. It's all good, brother. Just think of it this way: if you were a nine-year-old, six-foot-tall finger composed entirely out of your own DNA as well, then we'd practically be twinsies!"

I sit back down in the chair and rest my hands on my knees. I'm staring long and hard at a particular rivet on the cabin's floor as my mind struggles to assimilate all this new information. What sets this rivet apart from the others? Why is this where my eyes decided to land? What makes this rivet so goddamned special? And then I realize: nothing. It's just a rivet like all the rest. One of hundreds, maybe thousands, that hold The Pod together. One tiny rivet in a toolbox full of hardware. The fact that I ended up staring at this one particular rivet, out of all the rivets in this ship, means absolutely nothing at all.

"It just seems so unreal," I finally say, exhaling audibly.

"Believe it, dude. This is happening. And let me tell you, being cloned from a piece of dead flesh into a living, breathing, conscious being is not the most pleasant experience in the world."

"I – I'm sorry," I stammer, looking Finger in his gray-black eyes.

The living digit slides into the chair next to mine and puts his stumpy, misshapen hand on my slouched shoulder.

"Look, Abner, I don't want you beating yourself up over here. Before a few moments ago, I didn't even exist. Well, I mean, I suppose I existed as a severed finger, but I was not *aware* that I was a severed finger. Severed fingers don't usually have very many thoughts. No brains. No cognizance. Without consciousness, I was not. With consciousness, I now am. Abner, it was *you* who gave me that gift. You gave me the Universe. You gave me EVERYTHING! If anything, I should be the one thanking you."

He gives my shoulder a tender squeeze. I look up at him and our eyes lock.

"Thank you."

I reach out and touch him. Run my own fingers along the deep, sullied ridges of his knuckled back. He blinks slowly.

"You know," he says, "my sense of touch is extraordinary. I suppose that's what happens when you're a giant finger. I'm more in 'touch' with touch, I guess you could say. Hehehe."

I place one of my own tiny fingers on his cuticle and drag it from one side of his nape to the other. His eyes roll back in his head.

"When you place your fingers on me like that, the *sensation*...it's just overwhelming. There's just something carnal about it. Something raw and passionate. I can feel it in the pulse on the tip of your thumb."

"I wouldn't know," I solemnly say. "I've never been touched like that."

Finger turns to me then, almost seeming to blush, a subtle touch of pink coloring his wrinkled, death gray countenance. His mouth hangs open, just a tiny bit, as his eyes stare deep into mine. Am I looking at myself? Someone else? Am I even me? Was I ever me? Finger leans in and our lips connect. Warm and satiny, they feel, and when I apply pressure they apply pressure back. The breath through his nose tickles my cheek. So *this* is what it feels like to kiss! The smell of spoiled meat seems to fade away as all my senses are rerouted into my mouth. Our tongues touch. I grab him by the waist knuckle on his back as he slides off the chair and onto the floor. Our kissing becomes more sensual, even slightly violent, as we struggle to resist completely consuming each other. His stumpy arms slide down my chest to unhook my belt.

"Is this really happening?" I ask, my voice wavering a bit with both trepidation and excitement.

Finger just smiles as he slips my unsheathed penis into one of his rotten wound holes.

CHAPTER FOURTEEN

"I wonder if what we just did would be considered masturbation, straight sex, gay sex, or some new, previously unknown option," Finger muses, reclining on my cot. I lie there next to him, one leg draped over his wrinkled waist, my own fingers finding home in the crevices of his skin. The yellowing fingernail on top of his head scratches against the wall behind us.

"I wish I had a cigarette," I say, cozying up against Finger's shoulder, my head in the folds of his knuckle joint.

"A cigarette? Abner, you don't smoke."

"Yeah, I know," I say. "But I never had sex before, either. Not with another human being, at least. I saw this movie once and there was this guy and this girl and they had sex and then when they were done, they both smoked cigarettes. And now that I've had sex, I want one too."

"First off, I don't know if I would consider myself a 'human being.' If anything, I'm more of a monstrous unholy abomination..." Finger trails off, looking away.

"Hey! Don't say that," I tell the digit. "You're no more of an abomination than I am. After all, what do you think it is that makes someone human? Is it their appearance? Their genetic makeup? Or something else? Shit, Finger, it was 'humans' that sent me out here, into space, all alone. It was 'humans' who raised me to be their tool, a surrogate extension of themselves, much like a finger myself. 'Humans' cast me off their planet. Sent me away from their world. They sacrificed me to save themselves. And, at first, I was okay with that. Perhaps I still considered myself one of them, ya know? Because we looked alike and talked alike. I let myself become what they modeled me to be. Happily, I was their utensil. That is, until now. Until I met you. Finger, what we just shared, it has truly opened my eyes." I place one hand on Finger's chest and another on my own. "It's our hearts that make us human. Everything else is just...a coat of paint."

"Wow, Abner, I don't know what to say to all that..."

I kiss him on the cheek. "What was the second thing?" I ask.

"Huh?"

"Before, you said 'first off,' implying you had a second point to make. Just wondering what it was."

"Oh," says Finger, "It's just...I was gonna say that whether we're human or not, we *are*, aren't we? We're here. Together. In this moment. Right now. In the end, that's all that really matters."

CHAPTER FIFTEEN

After that, things got domestic for a while, Finger and I settling quite comfortably into the formal roles of man and wife-man-extremity.

The days pass as days do, as days in the past have done before, trickling by with the ease of a lazy river. Days of contentment. Days of white noise. Days that feel like memories before they even happen. Each morning Finger and I wake, eat a meal of reconstituted fishsticks and orange juice, and then make sweet love on the sill of the large portside window. Outside, the twist and swirl of distant galaxies casts the Universe in Technicolor. A crayon box of light, of wonder, for the two of us and the two of us alone.

"All of this is now ours," Finger says one day, motioning with his misshapen hand towards the stars. We're lying post-coital up against the cool porthole glass. He runs his own fingers through my hair. I sit up a bit and look out at the vast spacescape and I sigh.

"Not all of it," I pensively reply.

"Abner, what is up with you? You've been acting strange lately."

"Nothing. Nothing's up."

"You can't fool me, Abner," Finger says. "I know that tone. You've got something on your mind. You're sad."

"I told you, Finger, it's nothing."

"You're *still* thinking about Earth, aren't you?"

I shrug.

"Abner, how long are you going to pine for this lost world?" he asks. "Tell me, what good has Earth ever done for you? When are you gonna give it up? Let it go?"

"I can't help it," I say. "I know, it's stupid. As far as we've come, as long as we've been away, as much as they've forsaken me and as much as I've

ME & ME & ME & ME & ME & ME & ME & ME

forsaken them, I know – deep down, I can't escape it. I can't escape my own past. My roots. My story. No matter how far I'm cast, no matter how far we run, I will always remain their martyr. I'm still a man, Finger. An Earth man. And I always will be."

The severed digit scoffs and turns away.

"Don't act so high and mighty," I say to Finger. "Discount it as much as you like, but in some small way, you're a part of them too."

"Am I, though?" Finger goes. "I am an abstraction of you and you are an abstraction of them and they are an abstraction of the Universe. In that way, the further we get from mankind, the closer we get to the source."

"It doesn't matter, Finger. The prism of my experience is the only prism I'm afforded. We can run forever. We could run to the most faraway planet imaginable and still I wouldn't be able to shake the memory of home, rose-tinted or not. Like a cancer, the thought of home eats away at me. As much as we've been through together, Finger, I can't shake the feeling that loving you is only akin to loving myself. Because you are me, technically. And can one truly experience all this great big life has to offer by loving only themselves? Thing is, I don't feel the need to go back. I don't necessarily want to return. It's just...not *knowing*, the mystery of what happened all those years ago, the *why* of it all. That's what's been bothering me."

Finger has gotten up. I remain prone on the windowsill, watching the extremity slowly pace around the room. We sit in silence for quite some time before he finally speaks.

"It really does bug you, huh?"

I nod.

He exhales. "Well, I did have one idea I've been sitting on for a while. 'Bout how we might figure this whole thing out."

I perk up. "Really?"

"Yeah," he replies. "But it's a long shot. And you're not going to like it. But I think it might help."

"Look, Finger, as much as I love you, I'd give it all just to know what happened, what caused the communications failure, what happened to my home world."

"All right, Abner," says Finger, "but for this to work, you're going to have to trust me. Do you trust me?"

"Of course."

"Then I'm going to need you to stand up."

I stand up as directed, the sheet I'd been wearing falling down around my ankles. Before the six-foot finger I stand, completely nude.

"Keep your hands at your sides."

I press my open palms against my naked thighs and face straight ahead.

"Now, close your eyes."

I close my eyes.

"And try not to wiggle around too much," Finger continues. "This might hurt a bit..."

"What?" I say, peeking one eye open just in time to see the giant digit lunge at me. Like the tail of a scorpion he strikes. The fingernail protruding from his head pierces mine just above the eyebrows. Deep into my skull. Thoughts like a broken filmstrip flicker before my eyes – moments and snapshots of the life I'd lived. And the life I hadn't. All the ideas I'd ever had come to full fruition – they blossom, flower and die in a matter of milliseconds. And then like termites coming at me from all sides, the gray grip of death slides over it all. Swallowing it. Swallowing everything I ever was, everything I ever could be.

Finger pulls up with all his might, forcing my skullcap to pop off, my throbbing, delicate brain fully exposed to the cold, filtered air of my congolmernment spaceship. I go to ask why, but my faculties have ceased to function and I only can mutter some rudimentary animal sounds. All thoughts cease. The gray fades to black. I collapse into a pile of impotent flesh on the ground.

ME & ME & ME & ME & ME & ME & ME & ME

The last thing I see is finger standing solemnly above me. And then there is nothing.

CHAPTER SIXTEEN

Screaming I awake, yanking my still-smoking head from the refabricator. My eyes are shot with blood and streaming tears and the phantom pains of a billion subatomic needles stab at my swelling, itching brain. My entire naked body is drenched in hot, crimson blood. Tentatively, I reach up and touch my skull, worried that I'll poke my cerebral cortex. Much to my amazement, everything is back in place – skull, skin, hair, everything.

"Dude, what the fuck?!" I scream at Finger. "I was dead!"

"Only for a minute," the digit replies, seated across from me at the retractable table. A sly smirk creeps across his face. "Cool your jets."

"What did you do, Finger? Why did you kill me?"

"Whoa whoa whoa, nobody killed anybody, okay? You're alive and doing just fine, so don't be throwing out the K word all willy-nilly like that. And I think I may have just solved all of our problems, so you *should* be thanking me, not egregiously accusing me of murder."

"What are you talking about?" I say.

"Look, Abner, how long have we known each other?"

"Well, in your current state, I guess about a year, year and a half? But if we're talking about when you used to be attached to me, then I've known you my whole life."

"Okay. So we're pretty familiar, yes?"

"Right."

"Well, in all that time, I've noticed something about you. You're obsessive. You've wasted untold amounts of energy indulging this existential and myopic notion of 'self.' Especially in the predicament we've found ourselves here in The Pod, being cut off from the rest of your species and all. It's your ego, Abner, that is driving you mad. You ask 'why me.' Why this. Why that. Why anything. But where have those thoughts taken us, huh? Have they gotten us any closer to your so-called 'home'? Have they brought you one modicum of peace or understanding?"

"I – I guess not."

"Fuckin' A right, they haven't!" Finger shouts. "So all I did was simply cut those thoughts right out of you. A little brain surgery 101. I removed a nice chunk of gray matter, stuck you in the refabricator, and stitched you right back up. Bingo-bango, good as new."

"You cut out part of my brain?"

"*Hehehe*, yeah."

"But wait, if you stuck me in the refabricator, it should've regenerated everything exactly the same way it was, right?"

"It did."

"So how is that going to make me feel any better?" I demand, incredulous. "What in the Hell was the point of it, then? I'm still going to be the same me. Think the same things. React the same way. All you succeeded in doing was getting blood all over the place and giving me a massive fucking headache!"

"Well, I suppose it's true that I wasn't *technically* able to surgically remove *all* of your existential angst, but I did manage to figure out a way for you to stop worrying about it for the most part."

"Yeah?" I ask. "And how's that?"

The smile on Finger's face gets even wider as he motions to something behind me. I slowly turn on my heel. There, sitting in the doorway to the cargo hold, is a giant bloody brain. My Brain, refabricated and reformed, just like Finger. More brain than man. A puddle of clear, syrupy cerebrospinal fluid spreads out beneath it, continually leaking from its myriad sulci and gyri. A face, bisected by the two frontal lobes, stares out at me stoically as I behold this monstrous...thing. Like a prehensile limb, its brainstem extends itself forward, reaching for my right hand. I look down at the ghastly, slimy thing, unsure of what to do.

"Well, don't be rude," says Finger. "Shake his hand!"

147

Uneasily, I clamp the clammy appendage in my palm, shaking it up and down in a congenial fashion.

"Abner," says Finger, "meet Brain. Brain, this is Abner."

CHAPTER SEVENTEEN

"I realize my appearance might seem a bit unsightly to you, Abner, and for that I am sorry," Brain says. "Not for my present facade, mind you – as I can only exist as I do and still be uniquely me – but for whatever feelings of repulsion my state of exhibition may be causing you. Yes, I understand that looking upon your own brain, especially when said brain has been inflated to such massive proportions, must surely elicit a certain amount of...horror. So you are forgiven for your shortsightedness, my progenitor. You are a slave to your inherent and simple mammalian prejudices and cannot be held totally accountable for your knee-jerk reaction to certain stimuli."

"Wha...what?"

"Yeah, he talks all smart like that," Finger says.

"I will assure you though," Brain continues, "my intellectual capacity has increased tenfold in proportion to my size. And I pledge to you, right now, my allegiance to the greater good of this ship and all those who dwell in it."

"Finger," I say, speaking over my shoulder, "what is he talking about?"

"Okay. Ya see, Brain here is gonna do all the leg work for us from now on. He's gonna use all that gray matter, all that computing fluff in that, well, 'brain' of his, to figure out what happened. Figure out where Mission Control went wrong and why our communications and navigation systems went offline. Brain is gonna figure out what to do and how to get us the hell outta here. Possibly back home. To Earth. Ain't ya, Brain?"

"*Aren't you*," Brain corrects him. "Your grammar is atrocious."

"Gimmie a break, dude – I'm a giant finger."

"That's no excuse for ignorance."

"I'da thunk it's a pretty good excuse for ignorance."

"*I'da thunk it?*" says Brain, astounded. "Jesus, you're giving me a headache..."

"You mean I'm giving you a *you*ache, right?"

"Um...I suppose..."

"Hahaha," Finger laughs. "Who's the dummy now?"

CHAPTER EIGHTEEN

I'm up on the flight deck. I don't spend much time up here. No need – the flight deck has become more or less the attic of The Pod. Full of cobwebs and old furniture and long-forgotten memories.

I sit at the controls, staring at all the useless buttons and knobs laid out before me like empty plates at a restaurant. All the blinking lights, all the beeps and ticks, levers, triggers, latches and dials – all of them just a gaudy show. This ship was never in my command.

It still isn't.

"Abner?" a voice calls out.

I turn to see Finger sticking his head up through the hatch.

"Abner, what're you doing up here?" Finger asks, observing the flight deck as if it were a portal to another dimension he'd just found under the staircase.

"Oh, nothing. Just...thinking."

"Thinking? Why? We have Brain for that now."

"Yeah, I know."

Finger climbs into the chamber and slides his way across the smooth aluminum floor. He plops down in my lap and I wrap my arms around his hip knuckle. His face next to mine, his rotten-meat breath hot against the side of my neck.

"Abner, you can relax. You *need* to relax. Brain can handle it. He asked me for some time alone, presumably so he can get to work or whatever. Had me roll him down into the cargo hold. It took some doing, lemme tell ya. Like flickin' the biggest booger in history! He's all oblong and squishy and shit, and he keeps leaking all this gross sticky pus-stuff out of those wrinkles and folds covering his body. Incidentally, we're gonna need to mop up the main chamber before that shit crystallizes and we gotta chisel it off. My point is, Brain is gonna fix everything. Brain is gonna figure it all out. Me and you? All

151

we gotta do now is kick back and take it easy. Enjoy ourselves, right? Just think of it this way, Abner – the rest of our time in space together is not an ordeal. It's a vacation."

I sigh.

"A vacation that never ends *is* an ordeal," I reply.

The giant anthropomorphic finger sitting in my lap frowns.

CHAPTER NINETEEN

"Abner?" the voice of Brain comes over the intercom. "Abner, do you mind coming down here for a minute? I need to talk to you about something."

"What do you think he wants?" I ask Finger. We're relaxing on the bed in my sleep quarters. He sits up and shrugs.

"How should I know? He probably just needs a hand with something."

I press the intercom button. "I'll be right down."

I exit the bedroom.

"Can you get us some OJ on your way back up?" Finger calls out to me as I make my way through the bridge, the kitchenette, the wine cellar, the humidor, the billiards room, the library, the art gallery, the ballroom and shuttle bay.

The door to the cargo hold slides open with an Aeolian *swish*. I am immediately hit with a wave of thick, sulfuric stink. A brain fart. I choke out a wheezy gag before I'm able to cover my nose. All the lights have been dimmed or broken and the entire room is bathed in the red glow of The Pod's emergency light system. Like fire. Or blood. Like how a fetus must feel in its mother's belly.

"Let me first apologize for the lighting situation," Brain says. "I realize the color red may be perceived as a bit foreboding to you. Culturally, the color red is more often than not associated with the presence of danger. Red serves as a warning – be cautious, be wary. A red flag, if you will. But I want to assure you, Abner, that the red light of this room is more utilitarian than symbolic. For some reason, I have found the red spectrum to be much more conducive to gamma and theta brainwave activity, both of which are necessary for the calculations I'm currently conducting..."

Brain motions over to the wall next to him. Hundreds of thousands of numbers and formulas have been scrawled onto the metal; mathematical symbols like hieroglyphics on the inside of the hull. At first glance it seems chaotic. Like the mutterings of a madman. But as my eyes trace the numerals, polynomials, and integers, I can see some sort of twisted pattern in their arrangement, although it's well beyond me as to its meaning.

"What *is* all this?" I ask, reaching out and touching the wall. The equations seem to have been scratched into the ship itself. I wonder how Brain managed to do that.

"I think I may have figured out why communications went down," Brain says.

Instantly I light up, turning to face the overgrown organ. "Really?"

"It has to do with the very shape of the Universe itself. I'm not sure it was properly taken into account when your mission first commenced. There appears to have been a flaw in the equation your scientists discovered in that Iraqi cave, all those years ago. One that may have been overlooked. Until now."

"So what is it?" I eagerly ask. "What did they miss?"

"Let me try to explain this in terms you'll understand: you've heard of the 'Big Bang,' right? That infinitely dense point from which all time and space supposedly originates? Traditional models suggest that when the Big Bang occurred, the universe spread out from there in all directions equally, expanding like a balloon. But I think they got it wrong, Abner. What my findings here suggest is that after the Big Bang first manifested itself, it didn't head out in all directions at once, but rather only in *one* direction, quite rapidly expanding from there. This would create a conically molded Universe, in much the same shape as an ice cream cone. Now think of it this way – the Earth, your point of origin, would be the scoop of delicious sweet ice cream on top of that cone. Yummy, right?"

"Uh..."

"Listen! The circumference of the cone on which Earth rests represents the normal passage of time as you know it. The Big Bang, the genesis point, would be the bottom tip of the cone where all the melted ice cream collects. Still following me here? So as the ice cream melts away from the scoop on top, we slide down the interior of the cone. We are that melted ice cream, Abner. We're in the process of sliding to the bottom. And the closer we get to the bottom, the tighter the circumference of the cone around us becomes. What

I'm saying, Abner, is that the further we travel *away* from the Earth, the *shorter* time around us effectively becomes."

"I don't understand what you're saying to me," I say. "Time is getting *shorter*? What does that even mean?"

"It means that when we left our origin point, Earth, we immediately began circling the drain. We're slipping down the cone. Back to the point where it all began. The communications system must've gone out as we passed some sort of chronological threshold before such systems came into existence. Abner, do you understand now what I'm saying to you?"

"Wait a sec," I gasp. "Are you telling me that we're traveling backwards in time?!"

"Indeed," Brain gravely affirms. "Exponentially, at that. Faster and faster we go, every passing second getting shorter and shorter as we tumble headlong into the heart of all creation."

"The Big Bang?" I ask.

"The Big Bang," Brain nods.

"Okay," I say, nervously running my hand through my hair. "Granted that *is* what's going on here, what happens to us when we finally reach the Big Bang?"

Brain thinks for a moment.

"Well," he replies, "I suppose we'll eventually reach some sort of event horizon, some sort of edge to the darkness, the point at which all things were birthed, the point from which there'd be no escape – and we'd be obliterated at the molecular level, picked apart atom by atom, and compacted into an infinitely dense point in netherspace where we'll ultimately cease exist – we'll cease to have ever existed at all."

"We're going to be killed?!" I exclaim.

"Technically, I don't know if I would call it *death*, but the outcome from your perspective would be quite similar. So let's just say, yes. We are going to be killed."

After a lengthy pause, all I can manage to say is "...shit."

"Now Abner, I know that was a lot of information to assimilate all at once. I can repeat it if you want, speak a little slower?"

"No, it's okay. I got it."

"Good to hear, good to hear," says Brain. "Unfortunately, though, this next bit might be a little more difficult..."

"What now?" I ask.

"I have a confession to make," Brain says. "I had ulterior motives in calling you down here tonight."

"Oh?"

"I realize what I'm about to ask you might come off as a bit uncouth, perhaps even barbaric, but our current circumstances are surely dire and I want you to know that I wouldn't ask if it weren't an absolute necessity. Please know, I am only asking you this with the greater good in mind."

"Spit it out," I tell the brain. "What is it?"

"I need your arms."

"You need my *arms*?"

"Yes, that is correct."

"To do *what*?"

Brain holds up his bloody, fibrous brainstem in front of my face.

"This tentacle works okay. For a tentacle. But compared to the dexterity of ten individual digits, all functioning in perfect harmony? I'd be able to work thrice as fast and ten times as efficiently. Let me ask you, Abner, have you ever tried carving a complex algorithm on the walls of a spaceship with nothing but a rusty nail and your dick? Because *that's* what writing with a tentacle is like. It's not easy!"

ME & ME & ME & ME & ME & ME & ME & ME

"What exactly are you suggesting, Brain?"

"Well," he says, "it worked for Finger and it worked for me, so it stands to reason..."

"You want me to cut off my arms and give them to you?!?"

"Of course not!" Brain quickly retorts. "Don't be ridiculous. How is one supposed to cut off their *own* arms? I'll do it for you."

"Fuck that shit!" I say, cocking the brain an incredulous eyebrow. "This is insane. Time travel? Certain death? *Amputations*? I don't have to put up with this crap. I'm still the captain of this ship. I'm outta here."

"Unhappily for you," Brain says, "no is not an acceptable answer. And I wasn't really asking anyway."

"Excuse me?"

"I empathize, Abner. I really do. The pain of having your limbs forcibly ripped off may be somewhat traumatic. And, of course, as with any medical procedure, there is always the slight chance of...complications. But our situation here is a critical one, Abner, and you are not in sound enough mind to be the leader of our group. I, on the other hand, am a giant talking brain. I'm obviously the 'brains' of this operation, so to speak, and when I tell you I need a good set of arms in my employ, then unfortunately I'm going to need to enlist your services. Whether you condone it or not."

"You stay the hell away from me, Brain," I threaten him with a raised finger. "Finger didn't bring you out here to play Civil War surgeon with my fucking limbs. Your job is to figure out how to get us home before we get sucked into that black hole or Big Bang or whatever the fuck it is, and you're going to do it *without* harming a single hair on my goddamned head. Do you understand?"

I go for the door. Brain's tentacle shoots across the room and slams into it with a horrific crunch. I turn back to the enraged organ.

"You know I'm not about to let you out of here without giving up the goods," he says.

"Move that disgusting medulla oblongata or whatever the fuck it is and get out of my way, Brain, or I swear to God..."

"God?" Brain scoffs. "You simple, simple human."

"Don't act so high and mighty. You're human too!" I shout.

Brain pauses for a moment before leaning in closer to me. Then, in a throaty whisper just barely audible over the roar of the ventilation ducts, he offers his reply.

"Not quite..."

In one fluid motion, his brainstem wraps me up like a boa constrictor, its tendrils taking hold of my arms. I feel the pressure, and then the pop, as they're torn clean off at the sockets.

"Abner," Finger's voice comes over the intercom, "don't forget the orange juice."

ME & ME & ME & ME & ME & ME & ME & ME

CHAPTER TWENTY

I wake up screaming from the refabricator once again.

"That *sick* bastard!" I shriek, my newly formed arms covered with throbbing blue veins, like rivers winding through pallid sands.

"It'sokayit'sokayit'sokay," Finger says in one quick breath, holding me close.

I move my hands, stretching all ten fingers. Making sure everything's grown back intact.

"What exactly is OKAY about it?" I demand, standing up. "That son-of-a-bitch ripped my goddamned arms off!"

"Huh," Finger replies, considering my point. "Well, when you put it that way, I guess it's *not* okay."

"This kind of behavior is totally reprehensible," I say. "That goes for you too, Finger. No more assaulting me to harvest and reanimate my body parts into sentient beings. Is that too much to ask?"

"Hey, look – when I lobotomized you, I was just trying to help, okay? And not that I'm defending or condoning what Brain did to you down there, but I'm sure he was just trying to help too."

"Trying to *help*?" I ask, turning to hit the button releasing the porthole shutters. Slowly, the thick metal shields part like eyelids heavy from a long night's slumber. Outside The Pod, a universe in tumult is revealed. Distant galaxies and nearby stars alike, all in the process of unraveling. They smear across the darkness of the void like paints across a palette, collapsing all around us as we skip further backwards through time. This is the Universe in its infancy – before Nature and Order climbed out of that puddle of antediluvian soup and demanded some sort of logic to it all.

Finger steps up next to me, his jaw hanging slack in awe of the entropic clusterfuck visible just outside.

"What is happening?" he manages to eke, just above a whisper.

"This is why communications went out," I forlornly reply. "We're traveling *backwards* through time. Waaaaaay back, Finger. We're headed straight for the Big Bang. And from the looks of it, we're not that far off..."

"How – how could this have happened?" Finger asks, his voice quavering with disbelief.

I shrug. "Dunno."

"How long do we have left?"

I shrug again. "A few days, maybe. Week at most."

"Well," Finger continues, "does Brain have a plan to get us out of this or what?" His tiny eyes grow wide, desperate as they gaze upon me.

"I don't know," I reply. "I was a little too busy being mutilated to really ask any follow-up questions."

Finger exhales dramatically. "So what do we do?"

"There's not much we can do," I sigh. "We wait."

CHAPTER TWENTY-ONE

On the agenda today: make love to Finger one last time, say my final goodbyes, try to not let the regret and profound sadness I feel drown me as I become unmade in the ethereal womb of all creation.

I'm lying with Finger. Our bodies are warm where my skin touches his rotten flesh. Our breath falls perfectly in time, our heartbeats synchronized as if we were conjoined. Like we were one untainted entity once again. One body. I suppose this whole trip has been a metaphor or something like that. I'm not particularly good at articulating these kinds of things. Something about putting the pieces back together. Or finding yourself. Or carrying on...

That sounds profound enough, right?

"Abner, I need you down here again," Brain's voice suddenly comes over the intercom. I sit up, startled, and look over at Finger. The digit merely shrugs.

"Are you out of your goddamned mind?" I shout into the wall unit. "I'm not coming anywhere near you! In fact, I'm in the middle of having my final thoughts up here and I'm trying to make them heartfelt and erudite and shit and you're fucking it all up!"

"Jeez, Abner, will you ever stop with all this bemoaning, melancholy nonsense? *Why me? Why me?* No one is coming to your pity party. Now change out of your wet diaper and get your ass down here. I have a surprise for you."

"No way," I say.

After a brief pause Brain asks, "Is this because of last time?"

"Yes!" I shout. "Yes, it's because of last time!"

"You think I *liked* ripping your arms off?" Brain asks. "Hardly. I did what needed to be done is all. And now, we're about to reap the fruits of your most gracious sacrifice."

"What are you talking about?"

161

Danger_Slater

"I have a way out of here, Abner," Brain says. "I have a way to get us home."

"You...you have a way to get us home?" I softly say as my eyes tear up. I look over at Finger, whose expression matches mine exactly.

"Yes, you asshole!" Brain barks. "Now come down here, please, before it's too late."

"And you're not going to try to dissemble me or tear off any more of my body parts or anything like that?"

"Of course not," Brain replies. "What do you think I am? A monster?"

CHAPTER TWENTY-TWO

The door to the cargo hold slides open, going *swish* as it disappears into the wall. The light from inside is dimmer, redder even than I remember it. Like this doorway was a portal into the center of the human heart, or a big, backlit bowl of cranberry sauce.

Or into Hell itself.

Apprehensively I step inside. The walls are literally covered with thousands of equations, perhaps millions, etched into every surface. Upside down. Backwards. Written on top of one another. Intricate algorithms, complex ratios, rambling measurements recklessly abound. If I didn't know any better, I'd say it looked more like the prison cell of a lunatic rather than The Pod's former cargo hold. But then again, who am I to judge, right? I'm sure Brain has his methods, and those methods seem to be well beyond my understanding. And if it eventually gets us back home, if it saves our lives, if it frees me from the lonely nightmare of these past 10 years – then I say let the lunacy begin!

Approaching Brain from behind, I clear my throat to get his attention.

"Abner!" he exclaims, turning to me with a jovial smile. "Welcome, welcome, my friend!"

On either side of his bilateral brain mass, an overgrown, muscle-bound arm has been fused. My arms. Well, they hardly resemble my arms anymore. They're three times as long and 5 times as thick – now sporting boulder-sized biceps and razor-sharp shoulder blades. Extending one of his massive mitts in my direction, I instinctively go to shake it, but quickly withdraw my hand after almost having my fingers bit off by the jagged, shark-like teeth lining his palm. Brain's hand snaps and growls at me, prompting me to take a quick step back.

"Admiring your old arms, I see?" Brain observes. "Don't mind them. I tinkered with your DNA – just a smidge – before attaching them. They now serve as both normal, functional appendages *and* what are effectively two autonomous attack dogs..."

Both hands bark in unison, viciously snarling and slobbering.

"Nary you need worry though, Abner, they don't bite. I think. Either way, I'm glad you're here. Not a moment too soon, might I add. We're almost at the singularity, you know. The Big Show. The End. Or the Beginning, as it were. Once we cross the Big Bang's event horizon, there's no turning back. We have quite a bit to do and very short time to do it in."

"You said you figured out how to get us home?" I ask.

"Indeed I did," Brain replies triumphantly. "Behold!"

With a grand sweep of his mutant arm, he directs my attention to the inert Qdoor, still collecting dust in the corner where I'd left it.

"That stupid thing never worked..." I groan.

"Oh?" says Brain, flipping a switch on the side of the contraption. The machine slowly hums to life, its previously unused components getting louder, louder and LOUDER still, approaching a crescendo as more and more of its mechanisms kick into gear. An electric razor buzz gives way to car idling clangor, which in turn gives way to the roar of a jet engine as the Qdoor continues to power up. Then, quite suddenly, a burst of light erupts from the machine.

A blinding, pale-blue tunnel emanates from within. Rogue arcs of electricity crackle over the top of the archway like neon pubic hair. The portal is fully dilated. The teleportation device has finally been activated!

I squint my eyes and peer into the glowing hole, shocked to discover what looks to be a mountainous desert on the other side. There's soil on the ground, grains of yellow and brown, innumerable like the stars that used to polka dot my otherwise empty sky. Small, scrubby patches of grass grow from the dusty ground and walls of corrugated rock radiate heat in the honey yellow sun. I can even smell the fresh, revitalizing air that's unmistakably of...of Earth. My God, I've subsisted on The Pod's recycled oxygen for so long now, I'd forgotten just how *different* Earth's atmosphere really is. It flows freely into the cargo hold now, so numbingly pure that I am frozen in reverence of my majestic planet.

"That's..." is all I can mutter as I fall to my knees.

"That's home, all right," Brain concurs. "Though I wasn't able to align all the minutiae up as flawlessly as I would've preferred. Believe it or not, we're dealing with some pretty fringe math here. The results can be somewhat shaky. And considering the time constraints we're currently under, I'd say this is going to have to do."

"What do you mean?" I ask.

"Well, what you're looking at is Earth, to be sure, but this is the Earth of the past. The mid-Cenozoic era, to be precise. And surmising from some of the fauna running around, I'd narrow that time frame down to some point during the Pleistocene epoch – maybe 200,000 to 250,000 years ago. Right now, through the door, you're looking at the Al-Hajarah desert in what you'd call Iraq. They called it the Cradle of Civilization, you know. This area. They say this is where modern man first began."

"The Al-Hajrah desert? Isn't that where they found the equation...in a cave?"

"In fact they did, Abner," Brain says. "This planet, this desert, that particular series of numbers – they were the catalysts, the causes, the reason we were sent into space in the first place. Without that, we wouldn't be here today. This brings me to my next point: who do you think it was, Abner, that wrote the equation there all those eons ago?"

"Oh my God!" I manage to blurt, my eyes throwing sparks of Roman candle revelation. Illumination washes over me as the pieces all slide into place, and for the very first time I can see the big picture. For one brief, beautiful moment, it all makes sense.

"It was *me*, wasn't it?"

"What?" Brain sneers incredulously. "Fuck no, it wasn't you! Why would you even take it in that direction?"

"Huh? Well...I don't know. You were setting it up like I was supposed to have this big epiphany or something. I just figured..."

"*I just figured*," Brain mocks me in a nasally voice. "Ugh. You see, this is exactly what's wrong with you people. You 'humans.' All pride and no logic. All balls, no brain. It's really unbecoming – something I intend to rectify once I return to Earth."

"I think you misspoke there, Brain. You meant that's something you're going to rectify once *we* return to Earth, right?"

"Uh...yeah, about that...I may have told a slight peccadillo before. Ya know, to get you to come down here."

"A peccadillo?" I ask.

"A fib. A lie. I've summoned you under false pretenses," Brain clarifies. "I know our history up until now has been a bit...stormy, and understandably so, at least from your perspective. I'm sure having your arms ripped off is an unpleasant experience, and I sincerely apologize for having to do that to you. But like I said before and I'll repeat again now, it was all for the greater good. Step outside your own ego for a moment, Abner. Look at it as a whole. In the grand scheme of it all, what does one man matter? What is one person's life in the face of true redemption for the rest of humankind? You are a small bounty. A pittance to pay. And I don't expect anything more from you than what the rest of your 'race' expected from you. They sacrificed you, Abner. They forsook you, forgot you, condemned you to a lifetime of solitude. Blasted you away and shut the door. And now you're about to get sucked into a black hole and die in what is arguably the most horrendous death possible. What I'm about to offer you is a chance to live forever. Not literally, of course. You are definitely doomed. But what I can do is give your actions weight. I could make your life matter. You can go to your grave knowing that your death was not in vain. And I know right now you're thinking what kind of offer is that? Well...it's a lot more than most of those sad sacks back on Earth could ever hope for. And it's a lot more than you had yesterday. That's got to count for something, right?"

"What are you talking about, Brain?"

"I'm going to need to take your legs, Abner. I know, I know, I told you I wasn't going to hurt you, but I lied. It was a shitty thing to do, yes, but a necessary evil. On the bright side, pretty soon you're going to be consumed by the very fabric of the universe itself and it won't make a lick of difference anyway. Of course, I know these last few minutes of existence can be a tad...macabre. Death is scary, eh? So in the interest of fairness and to help put your mind at ease, I'm going to be so kind as to give you a choice."

"A choice?"

"Yes, a choice!" Brain says. "Now what is about to happen to you is going to play out in one of two ways. The first way is thus: you're going to give up your legs to me freely, happily, with dignity and pride, so that I may attach them to my body mass like I did with your arms. With my newfound mobility, I'm going to walk through the Qdoor here and into Earth's past. There, I'm going to fix this whole big fucking mess we're in by selectively breeding the protohumans that are in the process of evolving. Maybe I'll tweak a genome here or refashion a strand of genetic code there. Whatever it takes to make these monkey men a bit more cerebral, a bit more intelligent, a bit more enlightened than where we both know they'll eventually arrive. It's my hope that by the time they catch up to the 2100s, by the time they reach that day where they would've blasted you off on this godforsaken mission of yours, they'll have *thought* a little more about the causality of their actions. Maybe they wouldn't have polluted that beautiful planet of theirs to the point of annihilation in the first place. Maybe they wouldn't even need to discover the equation at all. Maybe they wouldn't have a use for it even if they did. There'd have been no coup. There'd be no conglomernment. There'd be no reason to escape the dying Earth, because the Earth wouldn't be dying to begin with."

He clears his throat before continuing. "Now, there is one downside to all of this, but it really only concerns you personally. I realize that tampering with history and the very fabric of space and time may have a couple of unforeseen side effects, the most paramount of concern to you being that your parents will probably never meet. Or have sex. Or even themselves be born. In turn, that means you'll never have existed. Bummer, I know, but if you think about it, that's sort of where you're headed anyway. Still, it is better than your second option, which is exactly the same as your first option except that instead of you 'giving' me your legs, I'll forcibly rip them off you in the most painful way I can think of. Perhaps I'll split you like a wishbone. Or maybe I'll do one leg at a time, pulling it out its socket slowly, as slow as I possibly can, so that I can hear each bone snap, ligament tear, joint pop. *Pop pop pop* – like kettle corn in the microwave. It really all depends on how much time we've got!"

"So there you have it, Abner," he concludes. "This is your ultimate end. I know, even against your better judgment, you somehow thought it would all turn out okay. For what it's worth, I'm sorry you didn't get to be the hero in this story. But that's what I'm driving at here, now isn't it? Everyone's the hero in their own mind. You heard it yourself from Mission Control, all those years ago when you were so desperately alone – if you died, they'd all carry on. And they *have* carried on. They forgot about you a long time ago. You're a postscript. An afterthought. Abner, you're little more than a footnote in *my*

167

tale. You're *my* side character. Why don't you serve your purpose and give me your legs? Fulfill your destiny. Make a *real* difference?"

By this point, the tears are flooding the dry riverbeds of my time-wrinkled face.

"I...I suppose my options *are* somewhat limited..." I mournfully reply. "And it would be nice to know I made a splash, however tiny, in the face of this limitless wave of time and tide..."

"Yesssss," lisps Brain, his excitement plainly evident as his snarling hands lunge at my lower extremities. "And so poetically put! A wise choice, Abner. A wise choice indeed!"

He snatches me up then, and I can feel the hot breath of his hand-monsters against my body, the gnashing of teeth as they ravenously rip through my pants. Panting. Snarling. Maniacally laughing. The hand-fangs rend my flesh, cutting all the way down to the bone, my legs like a pair of ketchup packets being squeezed at both ends. Sticky, incarnadine blood runs down my inseam like sap runs down a tree trunk. It hurts, but I don't give in to the pain by crying or screaming or begging for mercy. I embrace the agony. I accept it. Like Brain said, this is the only way for this mission to matter. For *me* to matter. This is my final chance to redeem my otherwise pointless existence. I am prepared to die.

"NOT SO FAST!!!" a voice suddenly cries out.

Both Brain and I turn to the cargo bay entrance. There, backlit by the glow of the stairwell, stands Finger. His nostrils flared. His demeanor, austere. He chest knuckle puffed out in a bold display of defiance.

"What's all this about?" says Brain. "All of us body parts in a room together – it's like a family reunion!"

"Abner, don't listen to him," Finger says to me, his eyebrows collapsing into a parabolic arc as he speaks. Pleading. Hoping. "He's wrong."

"*I'm* wrong?" huffs Brain, affronted. "Hahaha! I'm a *brain*, you moron. You're just a goddamned finger. What do *you* know?"

"He can talk circles," Finger continues, ignoring the abusive organ laughing at him from across the hold. "He can subjugate reason with his prattle, his blather, his half-truths and guile. But he is *wrong*, Abner. Whatever he's saying, he is wrong. The mission wasn't a complete failure. What about *me*, Abner? At least you met me..."

"Awww, how cute..." whines Brain. "I guess I didn't realize it was happy-vagina-feelings-time in here, ya know, with the eminent destruction of the Universe and all."

"I know you've been searching," Finger continues, unabated. "This whole time you've been searching. What's the purpose? Where's the finish line? Is there a meaning to any of this? Well, there's no easy answer to that, Abner. Maybe there isn't even a finish line. Maybe it's more about *how* you spend the brief amount of time you have, and *who* you choose to spend that time with."

Finger pauses for a breath, then continues. "You want to know what I think the meaning to life is, Abner? It's us. Me and you. Together, here, on this ship. And that's certainly not gonna be the answer for everyone out there, and I'm sure it's not the answer you were hoping to hear. But, whether you like it or not, that's the only answer you're gonna get. Don't let this brain rob you of our final moments together. Don't let our remaining time together be spent in vain. It's all we have, Abner. It's really all we have."

Brain gives an exaggerated yawn, feigning boredom. "Magnanimous speech, if I do say so. In a different life, Finger, you would've made a brilliant orator. *Ahem* Did I say 'orator'? I meant 'nose-picker.' Look, I wasn't going to destroy you, Finger, because you and I have a lot in common. We're cut from the same cloth, as they say. Or, in this case, the same carcass. But since you decided to be a big buttinski, I suppose I'll have to tear you to pieces just like this imbecile over here."

"Over my dead body!" Finger shouts.

Brain sighs heavily. "Have it your way, then..."

Still holding me by my mangled legs, he swipes his free hand at Finger. The dexterous digit dodges just in time, tumbling out of harm's way like an acrobat. Brain's palm growls a low, ferocious growl – all teeth, throat and saliva – a growl not unlike the incessant engine of the Qdoor. Like the refabricator making fishsticks and orange juice for dinner. Like the crunch and crumble of galaxies collapsing into the Big Bang's insatiable maw, just outside our tiny casket.

A clenched fist comes crashing down.

SCHWHAAAM!!!

Finger springs up just before the hand connects, giving a painful yelp as it bounces off the titanium hull. He charges Brain like a kamikaze pilot as the monstrous, whimpering arm swings back around, gaining momentum as it cuts through the stale, fetid air of the cargo hold. And then, just as it's about to connect, just as it's about to crash into Finger with wrecking ball force, his tri-knuckled body ducks down and leaps forward – prone, outstretched as straight as an arrow – straining his arthritic joints to their absolute limit.

Not even a moment before he's struck down in midair, chomped in half by the attack dog hand, the very tip of Finger's nail scratches Brain's frontal lobe. The latter's face scrunches up like he just ate a lemon, his arms convulsing like they just bit a live wire.

"Wha...what the HELL was that?" Brain gasps weakly, regaining his composure. "Don..don't you dare..."

Finger pokes him again, this time in the temporal lobe. Brain's hands reflexively shoot up in the air, releasing their iron grip on me. I fall out of their grasp and land with a thud on the floor.

"You...you son-of-a-bitch..." Brain snarls at Finger. "You knock that off!"

Ignoring his pleas, Finger pokes him yet again. This time Brain tics for a good fifteen seconds, his face twisted up in pain, both arms flailing like headless snakes. When the seizure finally passes, both hands at his side turn to him and growl.

"Uh-oh," Finger says. "Looks like your arms don't like that very much..."

He pokes Brain again, this time really digging into the spongy cerebellum.

"Ass-h-o-l-e!" Brain gurgles, fighting for control of his motor functions. But it's no use. As he writhes and quakes, his twin attack hands regard him with even more malevolence. Brain eyes the pair of snarling, vicious arms

170

nervously. He's losing control. The convulsions subside and Brain turns to angrily address his antagonized arms.

"Oh, just shut UP already, would you? You stupid goddamned hands! I know it's uncomfortable, okay? I can feel it too. But it's not my fucking fault. Have you ever heard of a compulsory response? Huh? Of course you haven't! You're just a pair of stupid fucking hands that don't know shit! YOU do what I say – I'M the goddamned brains of this body! I own you!"

One of the palms suddenly snaps at him, but he pulls back just in time. A devilish smile creeps across Finger's face as Brain's eyes go wide with terror. For the first time since gaining his sovereignty a week ago, something resembling genuine emotion paints itself across Brain's wrinkled visage. Something unconscious. Something visceral.

Fear.

"Don't do it," Brain pleads desperately, his voice gone atremble. "Humanity needs me...*you* need me!"

"*We* are humanity," Finger says, drawing an invisible circle around he and I. "And we'll be just fine, thanks."

With that, Finger pushes his tip even deeper into Brain's gray matter, causing the slimy organ to violently sputter and shake. His teeth grind so hard they crack like chalk, spilling out of his mouth hole like rotten confetti. Blood seeps out of all the twisted folds that cover his convulsing body. And then – just as the seizures begin to taper off and Brain senses a moment of respite – his attack-hands turn on their former master. No longer content to suffer the whims of their intellectual overlord. No longer happy being puppets of this fleshy wad of tissue they'd been forcibly tethered to. The hands want what Brain wants, what Fingers wants, what I want – what is so quintessentially human yet so hard to define – a chance to dream. A chance to hope. They've had enough. This is the moment they turn upon their wicked overseer. This is the moment they declare their freedom!

Their fangs tear into his soft, mushy body like it were nothing more than meatloaf, ripping out chunks of purulent pink flesh and wolfing it down. This in turn leads to more cerebral convulsions, which only excite the ravenous hands even further. Gobbling him down with rare gusto, they start on Brain's occipital lobe next, eating their way up to his juicy motor strip. The bloody fingers lining both mouths twitch uncontrollably as they devour their own central nervous system, unaware, or perhaps unabated, by the fact that without Brain, they themselves will cease to function as well. A murder/suicide, if you will, or just sloppy work – I suppose we'll never know just what the hands were thinking, because it isn't long before they eat themselves inert.

With one final chomp and a triumphant roar, they both fall limp at Brain's side, just as dead and motionless as him. His blood flows across the floor, pooling all around me. Metallic and warm. Mixing with my own hemorrhaging, rejoining my blood at last.

Finger ambles over to where I'm lying, sweat dripping from the pores and creases of his brow. He cradles me in his arms and hugs me tight.

"It's over," Finger whispers. "It's finally over."

"Not...quite..." I reply.

As the ship gradually comes to a halt, Finger and I slide forward in the puddle of bloody tissue that had once been Brain, sloshing up against the opposite wall in a frothy pink stew. For just a moment, all is calm and quiet. Stationary. As if we'd spontaneously entered some kind of stasis – a snapshot, an instant forever frozen in tableau. Even these words, these descriptions and thoughts, though they seem to flow forward at a normal rate, from where you stand parsecs away, far into the future, they're actually taking millions, billions, TRILLIONS of years to form, process, and come to fruition. So slowly, it appears as though nothing were happening at all.

We're no longer falling backwards through the eons of time. There's nowhere farther backwards left to go.

"We're here," I whisper.

"Here?" Finger squeals, his eyes darting back and forth. "Oh Jesus, Abner, where is here?"

"The event horizon," I reply. "The Big Bang. The end."

The thunderous roar of dying stars echoes all throughout The Pod, an unending succession of booming fireworks, fizzling back into the same Big Bang from whence they sprang. And as we ooze across the threshold of all

172

space and time ourselves, as we slowly pass the point of no return, the ship itself starts to break apart. Dematerialize.

First the cockpit – splintering like a popsicle stick before dissolving into fine grains of carbon sand. As The Pod inches ever closer to its eventual oblivion, that sand is ground into smaller grains of sand, smaller and smaller and smaller and smaller, until it stops being sand at all. Until it becomes...nothing.

Nada. Nugatory. Void. Unmade.

The screech of twisting metal only gets louder as we continue on our spiral, the ship slowly disintegrating all around us.

"Abner, we need to go!" Finger shouts, motioning to the Qdoor at the other end of the hold. Its pale blue iris still glows just as brightly as ever, like a giant eyeball – the terra and tempest of my homeworld reflecting back at us, so close yet so far away. "The wormhole is still open!" he continues. "We're done for if we stay here, Abner! C'mon, we can do this. Let's go!"

"I can't," I tell him.

"What do you mean you *can't*?"

With a weak nod I indicate my right leg, missing from the knee down, little more than a gnawed stump. I'm bleeding out quick, but for some reason the pain has subsided; I've already cycled through the stages of trauma and shock. I'm now approaching some *other* kind of plateau...it feels warm. Tingly. No more bothersome than an itch.

Finger swallows hard, tears forming in the corners of his crusty, boogery eyes.

"Wh – what?" he stammers. "No! No, it doesn't have to end like this. I can drag you. I can..." He grabs me by the shoulders and attempts to do as much. A paroxysm of pain shoots through me as marrow begins to leak from the nub of shredded muscle and splintered bone that used to be my leg. Then the warmth returns, continuing up my leg and into my core, enveloping me like a loving embrace. Getting sleepy....

Finger attempts to lift me once again, this time slipping in the blood.

"No no no no no nooooo," he moans, still holding me by the shoulders.

"It's okay," I say, hyperventilating a bit. "It's...okay. This is...what it is. This is how...it...has to happen."

Everything's gone a bit fuzzy by this point, but I can still hear the din of the mid bay collapsing in on itself, still feel the violent quaking of our once impregnable Pod as the Big Bang swallows up still more of the ship.

"Finger," I say. "Go...through the Qdoor."

"No," Finger weeps. "I'm not leaving you here...I'm not!"

"Finger," I repeat, drawing my hand tenderly across his cheek, "This...isn't a neg...otiation. Take these...numbers you see – all the...math Brain's been...scribbling on these walls – take it and...write it all down. As much as you can remember...carve it into the...rocks, if you have to. Just...just make sure it gets there."

"I don't understand..."

"This has already happened," I say. "In the far distant past...back when the Universe began...there was me...and you...aboard this space ship. You need to...get this...equation back to Earth. They need it...to build The Pod. The refabricator...the Qdoor too. They need it so they can...send me on this mission. So I can...get lost. Marooned...stumble backwards in time...I need to...lose my mind. This all has to happen...in the exact same way. It *needs* to happen...in the exact same way. We need to...keep making...the same mistakes, again and again so that...I can...meet...you..."

"But...but..."

"Hurry," I say. "Go...now...before you're swallowed with this ship!"

Finger stands up. The tears are pouring from his eyes, running down his cheeks. His chest heaves in and out as he finally lets go of my hand. My eyes have grown moist as well, but I can't even muster the energy to cry. The warmth in my core has finally reached my neck, wrapping itself around my throat.

"I love you, Abner," Finger says.

"I love you too, Finger," I reply.

ME & ME & ME & ME & ME & ME & ME & ME

He gives me one last look before disappearing through the Qdoor, the wormhole instantly closing behind him. Like a television's afterimage, the outline of my lover, my finger, my friend, is all that remains. Eventually, that fades too. I am alone in The Pod once again.

But it's okay – my loneliness will only last a few moments more.

Starting at my toes and working its way up, the Big Bang slowly begins to devour me. Piece by piece, particle by particle, I am sucked deep into that infinitesimal hole of nothingness that somehow bore this all. It only gets smaller the closer it comes, swallowing my hips, my nips, and soon enough my lips. And as the tiny puckered asshole of the Universe closes over the top of my head with an audible *pop*, it's as if Abner Almond never even existed at all.

Now, to some of you out there, you might consider this to be a fate *worse* than death. To that I say this: at least in death you got to be alive, if only for a little while. But to be utterly undone? To be negated? To have never even existed in the first place? That's a whole different can of worms. But I'm experiencing it, right now in fact. And let me tell you – it's not as bad as you might think. Because when you simply aren't, the concern you once had for your own existence simply isn't either. And there's really nothing left to fear anymore when there's really nothing left at all.

I will say that through it all, right up until the very last moment, I managed to keep him in the forefront of my mind. My Finger. My one true love. The reason I was born. The only reason why I was sad to go.

And then I just wasn't.

And that's it.

The end.

The conclusion.

There should be nothing more left for me to say, right?

Right?

I mean, at this point the story is basically over. I should cease this narration and gracefully evaporate into the nothingness I've become. Seems logical enough, yes? I mean, this is the pre-Universe we're talking about here. Where I am right now? It doesn't even exist! Just think about that for a second: what was there before the Big Bang? NOTHING! THERE WAS FUCKIN' NOTHING, MAN! SHIT, YOU CAN'T EVEN COMPREHEND THE CONCEPT OF NOTHING, CAN YOU? YOUR PUNY BRAIN JUST WON'T ALLOW IT! What I'm getting at is that I no longer even exist – I never did. And if *I* never was, then these *words* you're reading never were, either. But here you are reading them. How is that possible?

It's just that, somewhere between where we began – waaaaaaay back on page 1 – and where we are right now, just a few paragraphs from the end, well...

...something *unexpected* happened.

You see, within that infinitely small space into which I vanished, the rest of the Universe slowly gathered as well, seeping backwards like post-nasal drip. Even the burnt-out quasars, husk planets, and dead galaxies populating the furthest ends of the cosmos eventually rewound their course, succumbing to the entropic pull of creation's undoing as the Big Bang packed itself back into that overstuffed suitcase that exists outside of existence itself.

And then somehow, without warning or provocation, against all logic, reason and odds, that infinitely dense point became just a little *too* infinitely dense. Perhaps the Universe just couldn't handle its own staggering mass. Perhaps it had difficulties coming to terms with the reality of its non-existence. Whatever the case, there came a moment when out of nowhere, that tiny, illimitable speck of nothingness had had enough.

It exploded outward with a BANG of unprecedented and unimaginable force. A big bang, if you will – *The* Big Bang, redux! And when all those particles that used to be my Universe exploded back into existence, the subatomic scraps of matter that used to be *me* exploded along with them, into a brand new Universe. All the electrons and neutrons and protons that used to be Abner Almond were instantly released, mixing in with the very soup of creation, gradually cooling, tapering, and sorting themselves into patterns, physics, and natural laws.

Soon those particles begin to form into things, suns and planets and asteroids and moons. They become alien life forms previously unknown to the last

176

Universe or any other, living and loving and laughing and dying only to release that energy once again. And through the aether that energy – my energy – goes, spanning all of space and time. Back and forth and back again. Constantly in flux. A part of it all.

Do you see it yet? Do you understand what I'm driving at here? Do you see the big picture? The Universe, all Universes, are locked in a cycle of endless birth and death! The Big Bang was not a single, myopic moment. It didn't happen all those eons ago. It's happening right now! It happened yesterday and it'll happen tomorrow, too! And in this cycle, spinning around and around forever, everything that possibly can be already is! Already was! Already dead and gone untold times over. Do you realize the implication of that? It means that at some point during this infinite loop of time, perhaps in several billion years or perhaps in just a few minutes, those particles that used to be me get to become a part of the Earth again! I get to be a dinosaur! And a monkey! A baobab tree! And look, now I'm rocks! I'm water! I'm air! I'm music! I'm every realized and unrealized idea, populating every imagination across the globe! I'm stars! I'm laughter! I'm sound! I'm God! And then, one of these days, those tiny particles – those very same particles that were sent away from this world on a mission to save mankind, that crossed unimaginably vast distances on their way backwards through time, that fell in love with their own sentient severed finger before becoming one with the Universe again – those very same particles will inevitably arrange themselves into a familiar shape. A familiar mind. A familiar set of eyes that will be able to perceive it all. Those particles will be blessed with the gift of consciousness as they experience the world, however briefly, once again as someone called Abner Almond – world-famous boy astronaut, born and bred in a conglomernment-sanctioned reproduction lab, created with the sole purpose of transporting the Qdoor from a dying Earth to the habitable virgin planet XJ4-111Z-1.

Of course, by the time I become Abner again, I won't remember any of this – how he was, is, and always will be a part of everything – just like you sitting there reading this right now won't remember how you yourself were, are, and always will be a part of everything as well. And I realize that some of you might find this notion a bit frightening, a little too unwieldy, too big to swallow – while others out there might take comfort in it. But really, in the end, it's pretty irrelevant. All the anguish and isolation, all the joy and appreciation, all the stress and the anger and the envy and shame and love and pity and pride and kindness and hope and beauty and amazement and wonder – all of these are interesting ways to experience life. Hell, it wouldn't be much of a life without them. But in the end, they're just emotions. And emotions tend to obfuscate the only real, unequivocal truth:

Danger_Slater

I am you am we am forever.

So although I'm about to end this story, I'm not going to close it by saying 'the end.' I'm not going to say goodbye. My love for Finger is eternal. Unending. My love for Finger is the very fabric of the Universe itself. So I will not fritter. I will not cry. I will not wave 'bon voyage' as we sink into the depths of this endless sea. Today, I am. Tomorrow, I'm not. In circles around this carousel we go.

I'll see you all the next time around.

ROOSTER REPUBLIC PRESS

www.roosterrepublicpress.com

Tall Tales with Short Cocks Vol. 1 ~ Various

Rooster Republic's flagship anthology series. Featuring "Zeitgeist" by Arthur Graham, "The Night of the Walrus" by Gabino Iglesias, and "Mouse Trap" by Wol-vriey. Long live the short cock!

Tall Tales with Short Cocks Vol. 2 ~ Various

Rooster Republic's flagship anthology series. Featuring "The Apple of My iPhone" by Danger Slater, "Laser Tits" by Justin Grimbol, and "The Interstellar Quest for Snack Cakes" by Patrick D'Orazio. Cocks of the world, unite!

Tall Tales with Short Cocks Vol. 3 ~ Various

Rooster Republic's flagship anthology series. Featuring "The Lycanthropic Air Conditioning Folly" by Jon Konrath, "From God's Ass to Your Mouth" by D.F. Noble, and "Vasectomy" by D. Harlan Wilson. The cock shall rise again!

Grudge Punk ~ John McNee

Grudgehaven: "A city lost to the darkness, where acid rain drums on a hundred thousand corrugated iron rooftops and cold, mechanized eyeballs squint out of every filth-smeared window." From the twisted mind of author John McNee come nine tales of brutality and betrayal from a city like no other.

Editorial ~ Arthur Graham

Follow the editor and his client into the infinite ring of Ouroboros, the self-devouring, in this episodic novella by Arthur Graham. A story told through concentric circles of narrative, each one adding a layer of truth while further smothering all notions of certainty, *Editorial* will leave readers wondering just how many times the same tale can be swallowed....

DoG ~ Matt Hlinak

Culann Riordan was a high school English teacher with poor impulse control and a taste for liquor. He fled to Alaska before the state could yank his teaching certificate and toss him in jail. He hires on as a commercial fisherman aboard the Orthrus, a dingy vessel crewed by a colorful assortment of outcasts seeking their fortune beyond the reaches of civilization. As he struggles to learn how to survive the rigors of life at sea and the abuses of the crew, he fishes a mysterious orb out of the depths of the ocean and comes into conflict with the diabolical captain.

Texas Biker Zombies ~ Etienne DeForest

Have you ever wanted to survive the zombie apocalypse as a coked-out, white trash sociopath? If so, please look elsewhere—you will never survive Etienne Guerin DeForest's completely tasteless, offensive, and downright awful *Texas Biker Zombies From Outer Space*.

Alice's Adventures in Steamland ~ Wol-vriey

The American Queendoms of New York and Texas square off in this Steampunk Bizarro extravaganza! When war erupts between Victoria Queen of Hearts and Her Majesty Mech-Anna, it sets them down a path of intrigue and violence that threatens to annihilate both dominions. With the help of Lord Busybody and his mechanical assistant Crank, Alice Sin—prostitute/assassin for hire—may be their only hope to fulfill the 'United States' prophecy.

Chainsaw Cop Corpse ~ Wol-vriey

Simon is having a bad fucking week. When you're a D.C. Detective, every week is a bad week, but this week has been a BAD fucking week. For starters, some psychopath has been murdering people, stealing their body parts and smearing their corpses with peanut butter. To make matters worse, the contract killer "Boots" has recently resurfaced, and his girlfriend's chainsaw arm destroyed his bed when he made her climax. And if that weren't bad enough, now he really has to take a shit!

The Bad Ass Bible ~ Harry F. Kane

The Bad Ass Bible: The Bible's Greatest Hits Remixed encompasses a swirling, acid-trip fusion of biblical stories retold within the context of 20th century film, music, and literature. Moses is R.P. McMurphy, Abraham is Bilbo Baggins, and Jesus is (among other things) a kinder, gentler version of John Rambo. Lazurus digs himself out of the grave in true *Night of the Living Dead* fashion, while Lot and his daughters spend quality time in a post-apocalyptic, Mad Maxian future.

Voltaire's Adventures Before Candide ~ Martin D. Gibbs

Do you sometimes sit there, in your chair, wondering what it all means? Why are we even upon this planet? What insane person decided to place us here and give us these meaningless, hopeless, idiotic chores to complete? As if we were blind rats in a maze of corn. This story will not answer any of these questions. This is a bizarre story about Voltaire before he sat down to write *Candide*.

30964621R00105

Made in the USA
San Bernardino, CA
28 February 2016